The rhino faced them, its two horns looking like daggers. Jake realized that this must be one of the new arrivals, one of the black rhinos from South Africa, for it was dark grey and not as enormous as the white rhinos he was used to seeing in Musabi. The rhino stamped its foot and Jake felt the ground shudder. He expected Rick to signal to everyone to run for a tree, and just as his stepdad lifted his hand, the rhino charged.

Jake heard Leona scream and saw her fling herself behind a big boulder, while he spun round and hot-footed it towards the thorn tree. He was vaguely aware of Mr Cheng and his friends also scattering in haste.

'It's OK,' Jake heard Morgan calling behind him.

Jake stopped and half turned to see that the rhino had skidded to a halt.

'Just a mock charge,' Morgan said quietly. 'A warning to us.'

And that's when Jake saw the second rhino emerging from behind the bushes.

Also in the Safari Summer *series*

Pride
Hunted
Tusk
Chase
Howl

Other series by Lucy Daniels, published by Hodder Children's Books

Animal Ark

Animal Ark Pets

Little Animal Ark

Animal Ark Hauntings

Dolphin Diaries

LUCY DANIELS

INSTINCT

a division of Hodder Headline Limited

Special thanks to Andrea Abbott

Thanks also to everyone at the Born Free Foundation (www.bornfree.org.uk) for reviewing the wildlife information in this book

Text copyright © 2004 Working Partners Limited
Created by Working Partners Limited, London W6 0QT
Illustrations copyright © 2004 Pulsar Studio

First published in Great Britain in 2004
by Hodder Children's Books

The rights of Lucy Daniels and Pete Smith to be identified as the Author and Illustrator respectively of the Work have been asserted by them in accordance with the Copyright, Designs and Patents Act 1988.

For more information about Lucy Daniels,
please visit www.animalark.co.uk

10 9 8 7 6 5 4 3 2 1

All rights reserved. Apart from any use permitted under UK copyright law, this publication may only be reproduced, stored or transmitted, in any form, or by any means with prior permission in writing of the publishers or in the case of reprographic production in accordance with the terms of licences issued by the Copyright Licensing Agency and may not be otherwise circulated in any form of binding or cover other than that in which it is published and without a similar condition being imposed on the subsequent purchaser.

All characters in this publication are fictitious and any resemblance to real persons, living or dead, is purely coincidental.

A Catalogue record for this book is available from
the British Library

ISBN 0 340 87851 7

Typeset in Palatino by Avon DataSet Ltd,
Bidford-on-Avon, Warwickshire

Printed and bound in Great Britain by
Clays Ltd, St Ives plc

The paper and board used in this paperback by Hodder Children's Books are natural recyclable products made from wood grown in sustainable forests. The manufacturing processes conform to the environmental regulations of the country of origin.

Hodder Children's Books
a division of Hodder Headline Limited
338 Euston Road
London NW1 3BH

ONE

You'll have to lose the stereo, Jake Berman thought. He watched the girl walk across the garden from the guest chalets in the early morning mist, swaying in time to the music in her earphones.

The slight, dark-haired girl came up the stairs on to the veranda, nodded to him, then leaned against a pillar and sang quietly to herself with her eyes closed.

Jake, who was tall, with light brown hair and green eyes, shook his head and went inside. In the kitchen, he met his stepdad, Rick.

'Ready to go?' asked Rick, gulping down a mug of coffee.

'You bet!' Jake replied. He picked up the box of sandwiches and fruit his mum, Hannah, had left on the table.

'Anyone else ready yet?' Rick put his mug in the sink and took some bottles of water out of the fridge.

'Just Leona,' Jake told him. 'She's on the veranda, listening to her personal stereo.'

'Which, of course, stays behind,' Rick pointed out, echoing Jake's earlier thought. 'It's the last thing we want on the trail.'

He was referring to the Wilderness Trail that had just been opened in the Musabi Game Reserve. As the chief warden, Rick hoped the new attraction would bring even more tourists to the Tanzanian reserve, which would mean more much-needed funds for the park's conservation programmes.

Rick and his staff had been working for weeks to prepare for the first ever trail, which was today. Normally visitors went on game drives through the park, but now they could go on a three-day hike into the heart of the wilderness area and get as close to nature as the animals themselves.

Apart from visitors being on foot, a special feature of the trail was that it led through a part of Musabi not normally open to tourists. The area covered twenty-thousand hectares and started on the other side of the fence on the west boundary of the Bermans' garden. There were no permanent man-made structures in the wilderness area, and the only sign of human civilization was a small campsite near a river about ten kilometres from the main house. It was here that hikers would spend the nights in simple tents. There was also a rough narrow track that was more a game path than a road, to be used in an emergency.

Fourteen-year-old Leona Cheng, her father, Henry,

and two of his friends were the first tourists to book for the trail. They had arrived at Musabi from the Far East late yesterday afternoon. The three men were business partners, and over dinner last night, they'd told the Bermans about their ambitious plan to build a luxury tourist lodge near the game reserve. Before starting on the project, they wanted to experience a safari for themselves so that they knew exactly what they could offer their guests.

'Right then,' Rick said to Jake, going towards the kitchen door. 'Let's go and deal with the lady and her stereo!' He winked at Jake, his blue eyes sparkling with amusement.

Carrying the provisions, Jake and Rick went out to the veranda. Mr Cheng and his colleagues, Andrew Lin and Dato Samsudin, were there too, wearing khaki safari outfits and sturdy hiking boots. They looked at Jake and Rick with eager anticipation.

'Morning all,' Rick greeted them. 'Looking forward to hiking through the bush?'

Mr Cheng who, like his daughter was short and slight with inky-black hair, smiled. 'Indeed I am. It's all I've been thinking about for weeks.'

'Me too,' said Mr Samsudin, a tall, distinguished-looking man whose greying hair made him seem quite a bit older than his colleagues. 'It is going to be a great change from our city lives. And there is much I am hoping to see here.'

'Oh yes,' agreed Mr Cheng. 'And that is why

I brought Leona. I want her to see another way of life.' He glanced at his daughter and shook his head. Leona was tapping her foot to the beat of the tune that only she could hear, a dreamy expression on her face. 'But as you can see,' Mr Cheng continued with a smile, 'she hasn't quite left the city yet.'

That's for sure, Jake responded silently. Last night, barely an hour after Leona had arrived, she'd come over to the house complaining that she couldn't pick up a signal for her mobile phone. Jake had explained that there were no transmitters for miles around. The only hope of getting a signal was to go somewhere very high, and even then, it would be sheer luck to pick one up. Leona was devastated. How on earth was she going to contact her boyfriend, Lawrence?

Jake told her about the fixed line phone in Hannah's office and Leona immediately placed a call to Lawrence that lasted at least half an hour. Jake wondered what Leona's dad would say when he saw the cost of it on his bill. But then again, the Chengs were probably made of money. After all, Mr Cheng was about to build a super-luxury lodge nearby!

Jake had mixed feelings about the project. It would help to draw more people to Musabi, but did he really want crowds of people traipsing through this brilliant place that was his home?

Rick's voice interrupted Jake's thoughts. 'Let's get the show on the road, folks. Are all your duffle bags outside your chalets?'

The visitors nodded. They'd each been supplied with a large canvas bag for the clothes and toiletries they'd need during their time in the wilderness. A team of donkeys was to take the bags down to the campsite, along with other items like sleeping bags and food.

'I hope the donkeys know their way,' joked Mr Samsudin.

'Me too,' agreed Mr Lin, who was stockily built and wore thick horn-rimmed spectacles. 'I wouldn't want to wear the same clothes for three days.' Unlike Mr Samsudin he sounded serious, as if he thought there really was a possibility that his belongings would go astray.

'The donkeys know the way all right,' Rick assured them. 'They've been back and forth with their handlers for several weeks now taking equipment down to the camp.'

And two new tents just three days ago, Jake wanted to add, but thought better of it. Mr Cheng's party probably didn't need to know that the tents were replacements for a couple which elephants had gored one night! Rick was sure it was a freak occurrence and wouldn't happen again, especially when there was a camp fire burning. *They were probably just being curious*, he had told Jake.

Rick pointed to a heap of small backpacks in a corner of the veranda. 'There's one for each person. You can put your sunscreen, insect repellant, spare film, and so on into them. Also, your own packed lunch.' He gestured to the box of sandwiches and fruit, and the bottles of water.

Mr Cheng tapped Leona's arm. She opened her almond-shaped eyes and he signalled to her to stop listening to the stereo. Reluctantly, Leona switched it off and removed the earpieces. 'What?' she asked her father.

'We're going soon,' he told her. 'You must put your things into one of those backpacks.'

Leona glanced over at the rucksacks. She wrinkled her nose in distaste then half-turned to reveal the smart, bright red backpack she was wearing. 'I've brought my own,' she said.

'Wrong colour,' Jake announced at once while beside him Rick shook his head and said apologetically, 'Sorry, red's one of the worst colours to wear in the bush. You'll stick out like a—'

'Mobile phone transmitter,' Jake put in quickly so that Leona looked at him, the trace of a smile on her face revealing that she didn't mind him teasing her.

'More or less,' said Rick. 'You see, Leona, it's important to keep a low profile in the bush. As far as possible, we want to see without being seen.'

'OK,' said Leona. She shrugged off her own rucksack then opened it and took out various bottles of lotions, a tiny digital camera, a stack of CDs, a small mirror, and a hairbrush. She transferred everything, including the personal stereo, to the green bag that Jake handed to her.

Jake exchanged a glance with Rick who said, 'Er, sorry, Leona. The stereo stays too. Otherwise you'll defeat the object of the trail. Remember, it's a *wilderness* trail,' he emphasized. 'And that means getting back to nature – getting in touch with what really matters, and leaving behind all the trappings of our modern lives.' He turned to the three men, including them in the conversation too. 'Trappings like watches. While we're in the bush, we will move according to the sun and our own stamina. When we're tired or hungry, we'll stop to rest or eat. And when the sun is low in the sky, we'll head for camp. In the morning, we set off when the sun rises.'

Jake thought this sounded very sensible. So much better than having lunch just because it was midday. *Or getting up in the dark just because it's nearly seven o'clock and school starts at nine*, he thought, remembering how he used to force himself out of bed on cold, dark winter mornings in England when he still lived there.

'I suppose you want us to leave our mobile phones behind too,' said Mr Lin.

Rick nodded. 'Yup. Even your wallets. You won't find a thing to buy,' he added, a broad smile on his deeply tanned face. 'Jake will put everything in the safe.'

Jake put a pack of sandwiches, a bottle of water,

and a banana into his own green backpack, then went round with a box, gathering the guests' belongings. Mr Cheng peeled off his solid gold watch and put it in the box along with his mobile phone. In addition to his own watch and phone, Mr Lin had a pocket computer. Mr Samsudin tossed in his phone, wallet and an electronic diary. 'You don't mind if I take an ordinary notebook and pen with me?' he asked Rick. 'To keep a diary of what we experience.'

'That's a good idea,' Rick answered.

Leona took the stereo and CDs out of her backpack and, with a sigh, put them in the box, then unclasped her dainty gold watch. 'It's a bit like going to prison and having to hand over all your personal possessions,' she said, turning her face up to look at Jake who was at least a head taller than her. 'It's going to be weird not knowing what the time is.'

'I used to think that,' said Jake, who hardly ever wore his watch now when he was home from school. 'But you get used to it and then you feel kind of . . .' he paused, trying to think of a way of describing what it was like. With Leona's remark about going to prison still fresh in his mind, he said, 'Free, I guess.'

Leona frowned. 'Free from what?'

'Well, from having to fit your day, or your life, into a certain number of hours, I suppose,' Jake said.

Leona looked at him with wide brown eyes as if he was talking complete nonsense. 'But how else can you organize the day?'

Jake tried not to smile to himself. Leona had missed the point by miles! 'The day will organize itself,' he reassured her. 'Like Rick says, we have to get in touch with things that are real.'

'But time *is* real,' Leona insisted stubbornly.

The discussion was going round in circles so Jake decided not to pursue it any further. 'Anyway, I bet you'll have a great, er, *time*,' he said.

The pun made Leona laugh. 'I hope so.'

Jake took the guests' belongings into his mum's office and locked them in the safe. On his way out, he bumped into Hannah and his best friend, twelve-year-old Shani Rafiki.

'You sure you don't want to come, Shani?' Jake asked her. 'It's going to be brilliant. And Rick probably wouldn't mind if you squeezed in.' Normally, there was only room for six on the trail – four tourists and two guards – but because it was the first one ever, Rick had made an exception and said Jake could join in. He'd probably make the same allowance for Shani.

But Shani shook her head. 'Someone's got to keep your mum company.'

'What you really mean is, you're sticking around here to earn as much cash as you can,' Jake teased. When they were home from boarding school, the two friends often did chores around Musabi as a way of earning extra pocket money.

'That too,' smiled Shani, who was saving up for a portable radio.

'Well, see you in three days,' said Jake and he continued down the passage.

'Hang on,' Hannah called after him. 'We're coming to wave you goodbye.'

Out on the veranda, the visitors were listening to Rick's last minute instructions. 'We walk in single file. I'll be at the front and,' he gestured to a tall, strong-looking man who'd arrived while Jake was in the office, 'Morgan will walk at the back.' Morgan Rafiki was Rick's right-hand man, as well as Shani's uncle. 'Every now and then, the person in the front of the line should step to the side, let the others go past, then fall in at the back, just in front of Morgan,' Rick continued. 'That's to give everyone a chance of walking up front with me. Most sightings will be at the head of the line.'

'And try to talk only when necessary,' Morgan put in. 'We want to make as little disturbance as possible.'

'Last but not least,' said Rick, 'when we come across animals, do exactly as Morgan and I say. In most cases we'll tell you to keep still. But there might be times when you'll have to take cover behind a bush, or,' he paused to allow his words to sink in, 'even climb a tree.'

Leona looked concerned. 'Climb a tree? I've never done that before.'

'You climbed jungle gyms when you were little,' her father reminded her. 'It's the same thing.'

Not if it's a thorn tree, Jake thought wryly.

With the briefing over, the four tourists slipped the straps of their backpacks over their shoulders and put on their sunglasses and broad-brimmed hats.

Picking up his rucksack, Jake noticed that the flap was open. He looked inside and saw that the paper wrapped around his pack of sandwiches had been disturbed.

'Bina!' He looked around for the tiny antelope he knew was the culprit. 'There you are.' The unusual house pet was hiding behind a carved wooden hippo near the front door. She stared back mischievously at him, a lettuce leaf sticking out at the corners of her mouth.

'Thief!' Jake laughed.

Shani crouched down and softly clapped her hands together. 'Come here, Bina.'

Like a tiny pet dog, no bigger than a Chihuahua, the little creature emerged from her hiding place and trotted across the veranda, her jaw working as she chewed the lettuce.

'How divine!' exclaimed Leona, seeing Bina for the first time. 'What is that?'

'A dik-dik. One of the smallest antelopes in Africa,' Shani answered.

Bina looked up at Shani, and then at Jake, with big liquid brown eyes.

'Mmm. Butter wouldn't melt in your mouth,' Jake smiled, bending to rub the dik-dik's head. 'But you're a little fiend!'

'She isn't,' said Leona. 'She's a sweetheart.' She crouched down and patted the baby antelope who licked her hand with her velvety tongue. Leona was enchanted. 'I want one too,' she said. She looked over her shoulder at her father. 'Can we buy one to take home with us please, Papa?'

Before Mr Cheng could say anything, Rick intervened. 'You won't find one for sale. They're not souvenirs.' He sounded polite but Jake could detect an edge to his voice.

It wasn't the first time someone visiting Musabi had wanted to take a wild animal home. Not long ago, an American movie producer making a film in the game reserve had been dead set on taking a pair of lion cubs back to California. It took a lot of persuading, but in the end he changed his mind and left them in the bush where they belonged.

'But she's very tame, like a dog or a cat,' pointed out Leona.

'That's only because we hand-reared her when an eagle took her mother,' Shani explained. 'Normally, you'd never get a dik-dik to come anywhere near you. They're very shy.'

'Well, couldn't we buy this one?' Leona asked naively.

Jake exchanged a quick glance with Rick. Leona badly needed to go on the Wilderness Trail! 'She's not for sale,' Jake said, trying hard to be patient. 'You see, even though she's so tame, she's still a native

African animal. It would be wrong to take her away from her natural environment.'

'Oh.' Leona shrugged but Jake wasn't convinced she really understood. And this was someone whose dad wanted to bring tourists to Africa! She had a lot to learn.

'It would be a bit like taking a fish out of water,' Jake tried again.

'OK. I see.' Leona patted Bina again then straightening up, she said to Jake, 'I guess, I'm a bit like a fish out of water too.'

Jake felt a new sense of respect for her. Maybe Leona wasn't such an air-head after all.

Rick picked up his rifle that was leaning against one of the veranda pillars. He slung it over one shoulder, then kissed Hannah. 'See you the day after tomorrow, love.'

'Have a wonderful time, all of you,' said Hannah. 'And take care.'

'We'll be fine, I'm sure,' said Mr Samsudin, glancing at Morgan who was also carrying a rifle. 'We have two excellent guards to look after us.'

'And Jake's not too bad in dangerous situations,' put in Shani, winking at him.

Jake knew what she was referring to. Recently, a lion had charged the two of them out in the bush. For one horrible moment Jake had thought they were goners. But then he'd come to his senses and dragged Shani over to a tree. He'd shoved her up it and pulled himself on to a branch to escape the lion's claws by a hair's breadth.

'What sort of dangerous situations?' Leona asked, warily.

Jake gave Shani a tiny shake of his head to warn her not to go into details. The lion incident was something Leona didn't need to know about. The last thing they needed on the trail, apart from a personal stereo, was a scared tourist. 'Oh, you know, this and that,' Jake answered vaguely. Shrugging on his backpack, he set off after Rick who was already striding across the garden. 'Bye, you two,' he called back to his mum and Shani.

'*Kwaheri,*' replied Shani, waving.

With Hannah and Shani watching from the veranda, the hikers followed Rick to a gate in the strong game-proof fence that surrounded the Bermans' home. Rick undid the padlock, then slid back the heavy bolt and pushed the gate open.

Jake could hardly contain his excitement as he followed Rick through. This was it. The start of the first ever Wilderness Trail in Musabi.

TWO

Jake looked down at the valley that stretched below him. With the sun beginning to rise, the mist was lifting and he could see the team of donkeys picking their way over the rough, rocky ground.

'Do we follow them?' asked Leona, coming though the gate behind Jake.

Jake shook his head. 'They'll take a direct route to the camp. We've got all day to get there so we can cover more ground. For a start, we'll want to follow any tracks, like black rhinos'.'

For Jake, getting close to a black rhinoceros would be a highlight of the trail. There were very few in Musabi, or anywhere else for that matter. This was because they'd been poached almost to extinction, making them among the rarest animals on earth. All because their horns could be chopped off and used to prepare various medicines!

With time running out for the formidable creatures, Rick was working closely with conservation organizations to save the black rhino.

Recently, he had brought six of them, four males and two females, to Musabi from a game reserve in South Africa. They'd been released into the wilderness area and since then no one had spotted them. Rick said this was because they usually rested up during the heat of the day in thickly wooded areas and came out only at night to feed.

Jake had missed out on seeing the six new rhinos arrive because he'd been at school, so he was doubly keen on getting his first glimpse of them.

'Black rhinos!' echoed Leona. 'Aren't they dangerous?'

Jake nodded. Rick had told him that black rhinos could be very aggressive, much more than white rhinos.

Mr Samsudin was behind Leona. He must have overheard for he said quietly, 'Dangerous or not, I've always wanted to see one. And of course one day, our guests will also be eager to see such animals.'

Rick led them down into the valley, then up the steep hill on the other side. Although it had been cool when they started out, by the time they reached the top everyone was feeling hot. They paused to take off their jackets and jumpers and stuff them into their backpacks, then walked on again.

After a while, Jake stepped to one side and waited for the others to pass him, before falling into line again in front of Morgan. 'Not much game around yet,' he said, glancing back at the tall game ranger.

'Oh, there is,' Morgan assured him. 'You can't see them, but they can see you.' He stopped and pointed to the east. 'Look there, in that Marula tree.'

Jake looked at the tree that was about two hundred metres away and tried to spot what Morgan had seen. In the hazy light of dawn, it was difficult to make out anything. Then a small movement caught his eye and he was able to pick out an almost human shape right at the very top of the tree. 'It's a baboon.'

Silhouetted against the reddening sky, the male baboon was sitting in the topmost branches, gazing into the rising sun. Jake lifted his binoculars for a closer look and saw that the big grey-brown baboon wasn't alone. 'There's a whole troop of them at the bottom of the tree,' he whispered to Morgan. 'They're eating the fallen fruit.'

Morgan gave a low whistle to alert Rick. 'Nyani,' he whispered in Swahili, and for the benefit of the others added, 'Baboons. Feeding under that tree.'

'Oh, wow,' breathed Leona.

Jake guessed there were probably about twenty in the troop, ranging from babies to very big adult males. The one at the top of the tree was acting as a sentry. Beneath him, the troop feasted on the fallen yellow berries, shoving them greedily into their mouths.

Suddenly piercing shrieks erupted from the troop, shattering the silence of the bush. Through his binoculars, Jake picked out two adult males challenging one another aggressively. Lifting their top lips to bare their sharp teeth, they rushed at each other, squealing in anger.

Jake stole a glance at Leona, who looked horrified. 'They're not going to kill each other, are they?' he heard her gasp to Rick, while next to her, her father filmed the incident with a digital video camera.

'Probably not,' Rick told Leona, who did not seem at all reassured by his calm words.

The fierce encounter continued with one baboon chasing the other around the tree. A third male joined in, so that two were ganging up against one, kicking out savagely with their hind legs and sometimes trying to sink their teeth into their victim. Then quite suddenly, the battle changed. The two assailants turned on each other, their white fangs flashing like daggers while the third shot up the tree and barked furiously.

The rest of the troop seemed unfazed by the battle raging around them. They sat on their haunches among the fruit, picking up berries with nimble fingers and popping them into their mouths. Then, as suddenly as it had begun, the fight was over and the three combatants, all unharmed as far as Jake could make out, settled down to feed again.

The silence of the bush seemed even heavier than before.

'Ready to move on again?' Rick asked.

'Wait a moment,' said Leona. 'I'm thirsty.' She slipped off her backpack to take out her water bottle.

Her father and Mr Lin did the same and were taking their first swigs of water when the baboon at the top of the tree let out a loud bark.

Hraff, hraff. The urgent sound was as clear a warning signal as Jake had ever heard. Instantly, the troop was on the alert, chattering nervously and looking around.

Hraff, hraff came the warning sound again and now the watchful male swung down from the tree and set off across the ground at a swift pace. The others followed him, mothers scooping up tiny babies and hoisting them on to their backs.

'What are they running from?' asked Leona.

'Maybe they've seen us?' her father suggested.

'It's not us,' said Rick.

Jake saw that his stepdad wasn't even looking at the fleeing baboons but at something behind the troop. 'What is it?' he whispered and trained his binoculars in the direction Rick was looking.

Before Rick could answer, Jake saw it. The baboons' greatest enemy. 'Leopard!' he whispered hoarsely.

The big cat was slinking through clumps of dense bushes towards its prey, absolutely silent, moving forward with deadly intention.

Jake was so excited he could hardly breathe. To see a leopard was always thrilling because they were so secretive and almost always came out at night.

But to see one hunting in the morning no more than a couple of hundred metres away was incredibly good fortune.

Jake glanced at the visitors. Mr Cheng had his camera at the ready while Leona was staring into the bush.

'Where?' she asked. 'I can't see . . .' She stopped abruptly and Jake saw her go pale. 'Yikes!' she gasped, her hand flying up to her mouth. 'Let's get out of here.'

'Ssh!' Rick hissed. 'Don't anyone move.'

'What if it's coming for us?' Leona protested, not taking her eyes off the powerful carnivore.

'He's not interested in us,' Rick whispered. 'But if he sees or hears us, he'll vanish in a trice.'

Leona gave Rick a despairing look, glanced at his rifle, then back at the leopard that was coming closer and closer. His dull yellow coat with the characteristic black spots and rosettes provided him with perfect camouflage, and every now and then he merged completely with the bush so that it was impossible to see him.

'Now you see him, now you don't,' Mr Samsudin said under his breath. 'To think that such a dangerous animal can be so close yet be invisible!'

'He'll be coming even nearer,' Jake murmured. He calculated that unless the powerful predator got wind of them and changed direction, he could pass in front of them by as little as fifty metres.

Jake looked back to the baboons. They were still fleeing towards the wide and very full Chepechepe River that flowed lazily through the wilderness area and that had been almost bone dry a few weeks ago before the rains had returned.

Every now and then, one of the adult baboons stood up on its hind legs and looked back. Glimpsing its enemy, it let out an agitated warning bark then dropped back on to all fours and hurried on again.

Coming to the slow-flowing river, the baboons swung themselves into the massive fig trees that lined the bank. The branches swayed under the weight of the troop so that it looked as if they were being tossed in a strong wind.

Jake turned his attention back to the leopard. The cat was now so close that Jake could see the long white whiskers on his face and powerful shoulder muscles rippling under his skin. The leopard seemed to sense something, for he paused. Panting softly, he turned his head and looked straight in the direction of the humans.

Jake heard Leona suck in her breath and stifle a cry.

A fly buzzed around Jake's face but he dared not even to blow at the irritating insect to make it go away. The slightest movement that was out of kilter with normal bush activity could alert the leopard.

For a few seconds, the leopard looked suspiciously towards the group. Jake could see right into the piercing yellow eyes of the cat, as if the cunning predator had fixed his penetrating gaze on him alone. But the leopard must have decided that all was well because he padded on again, vanishing behind trees and shrubs as he headed for the river. Just when Jake was wondering if they'd lost sight of him altogether, the leopard suddenly appeared at the base of one of the fig trees. He leapt up at the trunk, hooking his strong claws into it, and climbed after his prey.

Chaos broke out in the canopy above. The baboons screamed in fear and anger and threw themselves from branch to branch and then into the neighbouring fig tree, desperate to escape the hungry leopard. Some of them even plunged into the river below, then scrambled to the bank on the other side and galloped away to safety.

A flock of hadeda ibises perching at the top of the trees suddenly took flight, calling out loudly. *Haaa. Ha-ha-hadeda*. The raucous cries echoing through the air added to the drama in the tree, almost like the soundtrack to a horror movie.

Jake was spellbound. Who would win the deadly game of cat-and-mouse? The tree that the leopard was climbing was quickly being vacated by the baboons as they jumped across to the next one, or dived into the river. But the leopard was undeterred. He sprang to the ground at the same time that a baboon dropped into the water. With incredible speed, the leopard pounced and landed in the river almost on top of the baboon.

Amid the violent splashing and ear-splitting squeals, it was difficult to make out what was happening. And then everything fell silent and Jake saw the leopard pulling himself out of the water on the far side of the river, the limp body of the baboon firmly in his jaws. Moments later, predator and prey had merged into the bush.

Jake glanced at the others. The visitors were staring after the leopard in amazement. Leona was very pale and her eyes were as wide as saucers.

'You OK?' Jake asked, hoping she wasn't about to faint.

Leona nodded, too dazed to say anything.

Mr Cheng shook his head in disbelief. 'That was incredible. I never dreamed we'd see anything like that.'

'You could spend your life in the bush and never see that sort of thing,' Rick told him. 'I've rarely seen a more dramatic hunt than that myself.'

Calm had returned to the wilderness. Looking across to where the closing moments of the chase had unfolded, Jake found it hard to believe that a life-and-death struggle had taken place there just minutes before. Even the other baboons had vanished, leaving not a trace of the encounter behind.

Silently, as if the shocking scene had left them

speechless, the hikers continued on their way. Every ten minutes or so, they changed places in the line as Rick had instructed. Occasionally they spotted some antelopes in the distance, or a small herd of zebra, and at times, Morgan or Rick would point out the spoor of interesting animals, such as the dog-like paw prints of hyenas, the surprisingly shallow indentations left by the massive cushioned feet of elephants, and the long cleated prints of giraffes.

Once, Rick stopped to pull up a clump of tangled vegetation that had stiff, spiny stems and bright pink and orange flowers. Jake knew the plant only too well. It was called lantana and Rick was always roping him in to help root out the horrid thing in parts of the reserve.

'Gardening?' asked Mr Cheng, looking rather puzzled.

'In a sense, yes,' Rick answered, uprooting another plant and wincing as the stem scratched his suntanned arm, making it bleed. 'Dreadful stuff, this lantana.'

Jake gave him a sympathetic smile. He'd had his fair share of lantana slashes too. He bent down to yank out a small plant that Rick had overlooked, grabbing it as low down the stem as he could to avoid the sharp prickles.

'Seeing as it's such a vicious plant, why don't you leave it alone?' said Mr Samsudin, watching Jake's cautious approach.

'Simply because it *is* so vicious,' Rick explained. 'Lantana's an invasive weed and it's not native to Tanzania. It was introduced here from South America. If we leave it, it'll grow so vigorously it'll start taking over the bush – and that would have serious implications for the ecology.'

'How do you mean?' asked Mr Lin, taking off his glasses to brush away a speck of dirt.

Rick bent down and wiped the blood from his arm on to his sock. 'The local vegetation is browsed by animals and in that way is kept in check. But the alien plants thrive because they aren't being eaten, so they soon replace the natural vegetation and upset the balance in the environment.'

Mr Samsudin listened with interest. 'It's a bit like introducing foreign animals that will compete with the existing wildlife in an area and eventually take over from them. Like when they introduced rabbits to Australia.'

'Exactly,' agreed Rick. A twig of the lantana bush had become caught in his thick blond hair. He pulled the spiny stick out, then continued, 'We need to think very carefully before we start interfering with the natural order.'

Mr Samsudin rifled in his backpack and took out a tin of creamy white ointment which he offered to Rick. 'Try this for that scratch.'

'Thanks.' Rick smeared some of the balm on his arm. 'What is it?'

'Oh, just an old remedy from the Far East,' came the reply.

With the lantana removed, they walked on, tuning once more into the signs of the wild.

'No rhino tracks?' Jake asked Morgan at one point.

'Nothing,' Morgan replied.

When the sun was high, Rick suggested they stop for lunch, choosing a spot under a tree high on a hill. Far below, Musabi stretched out before them like a vast green and brown sea. The Chepechepe River cut its way through the wilderness, glinting like diamonds under the strong, bright sun.

'Paradise!' sighed Mr Cheng, taking a long drink from his water bottle. 'This is exactly what we want our guests to experience one day.'

I don't know if I want to share Musabi with crowds of tourists, even if it does mean more money for the reserve, Jake thought uncomfortably.

He watched Mr Lin take a handkerchief out of his pocket and spread it on top of a flat boulder. Jake thought at first that it was supposed to be a tablecloth for Mr Lin's lunch, but he was wrong. Mr Lin sat on the handkerchief then took out another one and wiped his hands on it before unpacking his lunch and beginning to eat.

Leona also chose a rock and was about to sit down when a fat blue-headed lizard scurried across it. Leona flinched and took a big step backward.

'It won't hurt you,' Jake told her. 'It's just a lizard.'

Leona wasn't convinced. 'I'm not exactly keen on lizards,' she said and went to sit on a patch of short, tufted grass a little way off.

Jake and the others sat on the ground under the tree and took out their lunch too. No one spoke as they ate, content, it seemed, to be lost in their own thoughts.

When he'd eaten his sandwiches, Jake stretched out on his back and munched on an apple, staring up at the cloudless azure sky. In his mind, he replayed the leopard hunt, even hearing again the hadedas' cries. Then he heard another sound, a loud, high-pitched ringing, a bit like a mosquito. An electronic mosquito.

Electronic! Jake sat bolt upright and looked to where the noise was coming from. Everyone else did the same, surprise written all over their faces. Everyone but Leona.

Oblivious to the startled reactions around her, Leona was answering her mobile phone.

THREE

'Lawrence!' Leona's voice rang out with surprise and delight. 'You won't believe what we saw just now.'

But before Leona could continue, Mr Cheng jumped to his feet and was beside her in two or three strides. Not giving her a chance even to say goodbye to her boyfriend, he took the phone from her, switched it off, then stuffed it into his pocket. 'Didn't you hear a word of what Mr Berman told you before we left this morning?' he said angrily.

'I forgot to turn my phone in,' Leona began to explain. 'And anyway, I never thought it would pick up a signal out here.'

'Well, it did. And even if it hadn't, you had no right to bring it. Rules are rules, Leona,' Mr Cheng told her. He turned to Rick. 'I'm sorry,' he said, looking very embarrassed. 'I had no idea . . .'

'That's OK,' said Rick, although Jake knew his stepdad would be fuming silently. 'As long as it doesn't happen again.'

'It won't,' replied Mr Cheng, then folding his arms, he spoke sternly to Leona in their own language.

Jake thought Leona looked rather sheepish, and he almost felt sorry for her. He knew what it was like to be told off by a parent in front of a lot of other people. *But it is her fault*, he reminded himself. *She deliberately ignored Rick and brought her phone along.*

But even as these thoughts went through Jake's mind, nagging memories of the times *he'd* gone behind Rick's back came to him. It wasn't so long ago that he'd been in huge trouble for riding through Musabi on the back of a dirtbike without asking Rick first. *I guess we all make mistakes*, he decided, and to help Leona not feel so bad about what she'd done, he said, 'It could have been worse. The phone could have gone off when we were watching the leopard hunt.'

Leona shot Jake a greatful smile.

'Or when we'd caught our first glimpse of a rhino,' put in Mr Samsudin.

'Talking of rhinos, why don't we move on again and see if we can track one down?' Morgan suggested tactfully.

'What are we waiting for?' declared Mr Samsudin. He swung his rucksack onto his back then rubbed his hands together as if he was impatient to get going.

Mr Lin, Jake thought. *That's who we're waiting for.* Amused, he watched while Mr Lin carefully dusted off the seat of his trousers, folded his handkerchief and put it back in his pocket, flicked an ant off his arm, pushed his spectacles up his nose, patted down his shiny black hair, pulled a couple of burrs off his socks, retied his boot laces then, at last, heaved his backpack on to his back.

'Sorry. Are you all waiting for me?' Mr Lin asked, noticing for the first time the others watching him.

'Not a problem,' said Rick, his tone genuine. 'There's no hurry, remember?'

In single file again, they followed a well-worn game path down the other side of the hill. Directly overhead, the sun beat down mercilessly so that when they reached the bottom and entered a dense thicket of trees, everyone sighed with relief.

'Shade!' breathed Leona. 'Just in time. I thought I was going to die out there. Is it always as hot as this, Jake?'

Jake shook his head. 'No. Sometimes it's worse.'

Rick turned and said in a low voice, 'Sssh, you two. We're in a tamboti grove.' He ran his hand down the trunk of one of the trees. The rough bark was sooty-black and cracked in rectangular blocks, almost like squares of chocolate. He continued, 'It's possible we'll come across a black rhino here so keep your wits about you, everyone.'

A ripple of excitement ran through the group.

'What's special about a tamboti grove?' whispered Mr Samsudin.

'Black rhinos browse on tamboti foliage,' explained Morgan. 'And they also rest among the trees during the heat of the day. So we could suddenly come across one.'

'How could we *suddenly* come across a black rhino?' Leona murmured under her breath to Jake as they went on again, winding their way through the tall, straight trees. 'I mean, rhinos are huge, aren't they? It's not like you could stumble on one without seeing it first.'

Jake was reluctant to answer her because he knew that any sound could alert a rhino. So he simply shrugged, even though he knew that, like most animals in the bush, a rhino could easily melt into its surroundings and still be very close. *Like elephants*, Jake thought, and he pictured Goliath, the semi-tame bull elephant that often took Jake by surprise when he pitched up out of the blue on the other side of the fence at home.

Suddenly Rick stopped and beckoned to Morgan, then pointed to what looked like a heap of churned-up soil.

Morgan went forward and bent down to examine it. The rest of the group clustered round. Jake saw several beetles scurrying about, burrowing into the ground or pushing bits of the disturbed soil into balls which they rolled away using their back legs. Jake realized that he wasn't looking at soil, but at a big heap of dung! And the beetles were dung beetles, harvesting the droppings to lay their eggs in it.

'What is it?' asked Mr Cheng, sounding puzzled. He crouched down next to Morgan.

'A midden,' said Morgan. 'Where rhinos deposit their dung. It's a way of marking their territory.'

Mr Samsudin looked amused. 'You mean, it's like their private toilet?'

'You could say that,' smiled Morgan.

Mr Lin had been bending over the midden but now he quickly stood up and took a few steps back.

'Some of the dung looks fresh,' Jake pointed out, speaking as quietly as he could. There was a big reddish heap on the edge of the midden. Could a rhino have been there only moments before?

Morgan felt the heap with the flat of his hand. 'You're right, Jake. It's still warm.'

Leona stared at Morgan in disgust. 'Ugh! How can you touch that?'

Morgan chuckled softly. 'It's just recycled leaves and twigs.' He scooped up a handful which made Leona grimace even more.

'Gross!' she said, turning away.

Morgan straightened up and sifted through the dung on the palm of his hand. 'Definitely black rhino,' he said, looking at Rick, who nodded in agreement.

Now even Jake was surprised. 'How can you tell?'

'By the colour and the contents,' said Rick. He

picked a twig out of the dung in Morgan's hand and gave it to Jake. 'A by-product of a black rhino's meal.'

Jake turned the twig over in his hand. 'How do you know it's not from a white rhino?'

'Simple,' said Rick, still keeping his voice very low. 'Black and white rhino have completely different diets. Black rhinos are browsers, which means they eat everything the bush has to offer – leaves, twigs, shoots, the lot.' He picked a stick out of the dung. 'Indigestible items like sticks go straight through them.'

Jake noticed a white needle-like spine in Morgan's palm. 'And thorns.'

'You said something about colour identifying black rhino dung?' said Mr Samsudin.

'Yes. Sometimes, it's reddish like this.' Rick bent down and scooped up more of the dung. 'That's because of the sap and leaves of the tamboti tree.'

Although Mr Lin was standing some way back, he was following the conversation with interest. 'Amazing what you can tell from a heap of . . .' His voice trailed off and Jake wondered if the tidy looking man found the topic rather distasteful, but Mr Lin went on, 'If a black rhino's, er, dung, is red and full of sticks and thorns, what are the characteristics of a white rhino's droppings?'

'White rhinos eat mainly grass,' Morgan explained. 'So fresh white rhino dung is green and steaming.'

'And you wouldn't be so ready to pick *that*

up,' suggested Mr Cheng, who was standing up again.

'Probably not,' Morgan admitted. 'At least not until it's dry. And then it's a lot like straw.'

Jake decided he knew quite enough about rhino dung. 'Do you think we can stop studying the stuff now and look for the animal that made it?' he asked Rick. 'Aren't there other clues we can look for?'

'Sure.' Rick winked at Morgan. 'Rhinos spray to mark their territory, so you can go round smelling the bushes and trees.'

'Thanks, but no thanks,' Jake grinned.

'Or we can go by the scrape marks the rhinos make on the ground with their feet. That spreads their scent and tells other rhinos who the area belongs to,' Morgan added.

'OK, then. Let's follow the scrape marks,' said Jake.

'They're not always that obvious to us,' Rick warned. 'Our best bet is to keep walking. After all, we know there's a rhino about.' He pointed to the fresh dung. 'Be on your guard, everyone. That rhino's pretty close.'

Unlike everyone else, Leona seemed less than eager to see a black rhino. She glanced at Rick's rifle which he carried almost indifferently over one shoulder. 'Shouldn't your dad have his gun at the ready?' she whispered to Jake.

'He has,' Jake assured her. He was growing more and more impatient with Leona. If she was so lily-livered, why did she come on the trail? 'That gun can be off Rick's shoulder and ready to fire in a heartbeat. And Morgan's just as good.'

'I hope you're right,' sighed Leona.

Rick had overheard her. 'Shooting's our last resort. There should be no need for it if we all follow the rules. Keep close together, and try to step where the person in front of you has trod. That'll keep the noise down. And always be aware of where the nearest tree is in case you need to climb one. If it's a thorn tree, too bad! Better to be scratched by a few thorns than gored by a rhino.'

Jake heard Leona suck in her breath. 'And if there's no tree?' she asked hesitantly.

'Then you'd better pray,' her father told her.

'Or at least try to get behind a bush or a boulder,' said Morgan. 'Rhinos have poor eyesight and they charge with their heads down. If one does go for you and you manage to get out of its way, you might be OK.'

'Thanks for the tip,' said Leona, looking as nervous as ever.

Rick moved on again, treading so lightly he hardly made a sound. The others followed, but then Leona stood on a twig which cracked in the silence of the grove like a shot ringing out.

'Sorry!' she gulped, and glancing at Jake over her shoulder she whispered, 'I'm not doing too well, what with my phone and now this.'

'Just an accident,' Jake mouthed although he couldn't help feeling irritated.

Rick paused to pick up a handful of dust. He let it fall to the ground.

'What's he doing?' Leona whispered to Jake, coming so close to him that her lips brushed his ear.

'Checking to see where the breeze is coming from,' Jake told her. 'To make sure we walk into it.'

On they went, heading into the unseen breeze so that the rhino wouldn't pick up their scent.

Jake felt every fibre of his body straining to detect the slightest movement or sound. Was this what it was like for a creature in the bush, constantly having to be aware of its surroundings in case there was danger about?

But soon Jake's impatience began to get the better of him. He waited while Morgan scrutinized a mark on the ground then, when the assistant ranger stood up, he whispered, 'Can't we just track the rhino using a tracking signal?' He knew that the Musabi rhinos had all been fitted with transmitters which could accurately reveal where they were. Rangers simply had to carry a hand-held radio tracking device which looked a bit like a TV aerial and follow the bleeps the instrument made. The nearer the animal, the stronger the bleeps.

'That would be the easy way,' Morgan agreed. 'But it would be cheating. The whole idea of the trail is to be one with nature and to allow our guests the thrill of tracking an animal using the signs of the wild.'

'But this is the twenty-first century,' Jake protested, forgetting how critical he'd been of Leona and her twenty-first century mobile phone. 'We should be allowed to use a bit of technology.'

'Only when it's necessary,' Morgan responded.

Deeper and deeper into the grove they went, stepping carefully over stones and fallen branches. Every now and then Rick would stop and hold up one hand, and they would all wait with bated breath, only to be disappointed a moment later when a bird flew out in front of them, or a big shape just ahead turned out to be a boulder.

That rhino's gone, Jake decided eventually. *There's hardly anything else alive in this grove. We're creeping about like ghosts for nothing*. But the thought had barely left him when he spied a movement in some bushes about ten metres to the left. Rick had seen it too, for he stopped and signalled to the others to freeze.

Jake stared hard into the bushes. All he could see were leaves and branches. *False alarm. Again!* He sighed, feeling rather fed up with the rhino hunt now. He expected the pattern of the walk to repeat itself – Rick going on and the others following him like a pack of obedient dogs. But Jake was wrong. Rick kept absolutely still, his eyes fixed on the bushes ahead.

Maybe it's a snake, Jake thought and then a puff of wind reached him, bringing with it the rich, earthy smell of a wild animal. And even though he still couldn't see a thing, Jake heard what sounded like breathing – a deep drawing in of air, followed by a soft exhaling noise as the mystery creature breathed out. *It could be anything,* Jake told himself. *Lion, elephant, bushbuck . . .*

In front of him, Leona shifted her weight from one foot to the other and at that same instant, Jake glimpsed another flicker of movement in the bushes. The twitch of an ear perhaps, or a whisk of a tail. A new noise followed, a dull thud like the stamping of a heavy foot.

A chill ran down Jake's spine. If it was a rhino, it was incredibly close, too close for comfort. Without daring to move his head, he strained his eyes to see where the nearest tree was. There was one a couple of metres to his right. *A thorn tree,* Jake thought grimly. *Just my luck.*

The dull thud shook the ground again. Then came a snort and a low grunt. Jake was convinced that it was a rhino behind the bush. And it was about to charge!

Rick signalled urgently, and Jake read in the signal a warning to be ready to run for safety.

A suffocating tension gripped the grove. Jake felt it pressing in on him, making it hard to breathe, while the silence pounded his ears.

The tiniest rustle of leaves slashed through the stifled air like a sword. And then, right before Jake's eyes, a huge bulky grey shape appeared from behind the bush. It *was* a rhino, with its head lowered and ears pricked threateningly.

Jake heard Leona draw in her breath and he prayed she wouldn't scream or go dashing through the bush in fright. That would definitely make the rhino charge.

The rhino faced them, its two horns looking like daggers. Jake realized that this must be one of the new arrivals, one of the black rhinos from South Africa, for it was dark grey and not as enormous as the white rhinos he was used to seeing in Musabi.

The rhino stamped its foot and Jake felt the ground shudder. He expected Rick to signal to everyone to run for a tree, and just as his stepdad lifted his hand, the rhino charged.

Jake heard Leona scream and saw her fling herself behind a big boulder, while he spun round and hot-footed it towards the thorn tree. He was vaguely aware of Mr Cheng and his friends also scattering in haste.

'It's OK,' Jake heard Morgan calling behind him.

Jake stopped and half turned to see that the rhino had skidded to a halt.

'Just a mock charge,' Morgan said quietly. 'A warning to us.'

And that's when Jake saw the second rhino emerging from behind the bushes. But this one was as harmless as the other one was dangerous. It was tiny, not much bigger than a spaniel, and its back reached no higher than the adult's pendulous belly. It stared towards Jake and flicked funnel-shaped ears that seemed several sizes too big for it.

'A calf,' Jake breathed.

A broad smile spread across Rick's face. 'The six have become seven.'

FOUR

That night, sitting on cushions around the camp fire, the hikers discussed their action-packed day. They all agreed that they'd seen more than they'd bargained on.

After the mock charge, the mother rhino had warily watched the intruders for a few minutes. Her calf stood just behind her, blinking at the humans like a shy child peeping out from behind its mother's skirt. Finally the pair had whirled round and trotted through the tamboti grove, quickly disappearing from view. The hikers had gone on and carefully reached the camp just as the sun sank below the horizon.

Nyika camp was situated in a clearing near the banks of a stream. It consisted of six tents arranged in a circle, with a fire in the centre and three other tents at the edge. Two of these were for the camp staff, while the third was the kitchen tent where the camp cook prepared the meals. Paraffin lanterns hanging from branches provided just enough light for people to see where they were walking, while the central fire was not only the focal point of the camp but also helped to keep wild animals at bay.

'I don't know which was more amazing, the leopard hunt or nearly being charged by a black rhino,' Jake remarked, watching the dancing flames as he broke open a can of Coke.

'You can keep the rhino charge,' said Leona, sitting cross-legged on her cushion. 'That nearly gave me a heart attack.'

'What about the poor baboons?' her father asked. 'They must have been having heart attacks too.'

Leona looked sympathetic. 'I guess so. Poor things. Life in the wild must be very tough.'

'I enjoyed the buffalo,' said Mr Lin, referring to a large herd they had seen crossing the Chepechepe River. 'Because they were far away.'

Everyone laughed. 'You have a point there,' said Mr Cheng, helping himself to a beer from a coolbox nearby. 'But what a privilege it was to get so close to one of the rarest animals on earth.'

'Indeed,' agreed Mr Samsudin. 'Seeing that rhinoceros was like a dream come true.'

'To me, the best thing was finding a brand-new rhino in Musabi,' said Morgan.

Rick raised his bottle of beer. 'I'll drink to that!' He chinked the bottle against Jake's coke. 'To the rhinos!'

The others lifted their drinks too. 'The rhinos.'

'To Little and Large,' chuckled Leona.

Jake frowned. 'You make them sound like a comedy act.'

Leona's father peered at her through the firelight. 'You have the imagination of a mosquito, Leona,' he said, slapping one that had landed on his arm.

Jake laughed and Leona pulled a face at him. 'OK, let's see if your imagination's any better, Mr Creative Jake.'

'How about "Mother" and "Small Rhinoceros"?' Jake suggested. Then, noticing Leona wrinkle her nose in disapproval, he added smartly, 'But in Swahili.'

'That would be Nina and Pea,' Morgan translated, winking at Jake.

'Not bad,' Leona admitted. 'So you speak Swahili, Jake?'

Jake shrugged. 'A bit.'

'Seems a strange thing to do, name wild rhinos,' Mr Samsudin said. 'But I must say, the names fit well.' He stood up. 'I should be making notes of everything we saw today while it's all still fresh in my mind.' He went over to his tent.

'Don't forget to do up the zip again when you come out,' Rick called after him.

Jake pictured what could happen if the tent was left open. Certain snakes, particularly spitting cobras, were quick to slither in through unfastened tent flaps and curl up in a sleeping bag.

Rick leaned forward and stoked the fire with a long stick. The flames flared up briefly, shooting bright sparks into the night. 'We'll need more wood soon,' he said.

'Here's some.' Mr Lin picked up a fallen branch lying on the ground next to him. He was about to toss it on the fire when Rick stopped him.

'No, that's tamboti. The fumes can be poisonous. The camp staff will have stacked some other firewood behind the kitchen tent.'

'I'll get it,' Jake offered, jumping up. He went over to the kitchen area where the cook, Jackson Kupika, was preparing the evening meal. He'd come down to the camp earlier with the donkey train. The donkeys were now corralled in a lion-proof enclosure where they would stay until the end of the trail when they'd take the duffle bags back again.

'Are you hungry?' asked Jackson.

'Starving,' Jake said. A delicious smell came from the three-legged cast-iron cooking pot that stood over the fire next to the tent. 'What's for dinner?'

'Boeuf Bourguignonne.'

'Great,' said Jake. He pointed to a second cast-iron pot standing in the red hot embers. 'What's in there? Pudding?'

'No. Hot water. For your showers.'

'Oh, right.' Jake was looking forward to his first shower in the wilderness, mainly because he'd come down with Rick just last weekend to help rig up the simple contraption. It was basically a bucket with a tap at the bottom and a rope attached to the handle.

The rope was slung over a high branch and the loose end tied to a stake in the ground.

The idea was to fill the bucket with hot water, then hoist it up by pulling on the rope. Next, you tied the rope to the stake again so that the bucket was suspended in the air. Then it was simply a matter of turning on the tap and standing underneath the bucket while the water spurted out.

Jake imagined Leona making some cutting remark about it being very primitive, or even refusing point blank to go up the narrow path to the bathroom clearing. She'd already been horrified by the loo which was nothing more than a hole in the ground which people had to dig themselves!

Jake piled some logs into his arms then went back to the camp fire.

Mr Samsudin was back too, busily scribbling notes in his diary. 'Apart from their dung, how do you tell black and white rhino apart, Rick? I think I once read something about the shape of their lips.'

'That's right,' Rick answered. 'White rhinos have square upper lips, while the black ones have pointed, almost hooked top lips which they use for grasping food. And that's where the terms black and white come from. You see, originally the square-lipped rhino was described as having a wide, or in Dutch, *weit*, lip. In time this word *weit* became *white*.'

'That's interesting. I always thought it was because one type of rhino was blacker and the other more whitish,' said Leona. She was reclining on her cushion which she'd propped up against a rock.

Jake carefully put a couple of logs on the fire. 'Did that rhino look black to you this afternoon?' he teased. Hadn't Leona ever seen pictures of rhinos and realized that both species were grey, even though the white rhino was a lighter grey?

'Very black. As black as thunder,' came the reply and Jake grinned, sharing the joke.

'Hey!' Leona suddenly exclaimed. She was looking up at the sky, her face filled with wonder. 'I just saw a shooting star.'

'You did?' Her father gazed up too.

'And would you look at all the millions of stars?' Leona went on. 'Trillions, even.'

Jake had almost forgotten just how incredible he'd found the night sky when he first arrived at Musabi a year ago. Night after night he used to lie out on the lawn, almost overwhelmed by the myriad of stars above. It was particularly amazing on moonless nights when the black sky was lit up by countless pinpricks of twinkling silver lights, like a kind of celestial Christmas tree.

'It's as if there are more stars than sky,' Leona said in awe. 'And look, another shooting star!'

Jake had seen it too, the bright arrow of a meteor hurtling through the heavens then vanishing suddenly as it burned up in the earth's atmosphere.

'This is just brilliant!' Leona couldn't contain her

enthusiasm. 'Like a fireworks display, only a lot better.'

'Unfortunately, at home we have to be content with fireworks,' said Mr Lin. 'The light pollution from our city means we never see a single star, let alone a sky full of them. This really is a wonderful treat for us. Our lodge guests will love it too.'

Leona couldn't tear her gaze away from the sky, not even when Jackson came over with the food. 'This is definitely the best thing I've seen today,' she said, lying back with her hands behind her head. 'Now I really know that we're just a speck in the universe.'

They helped themselves to the meal, Jake serving up a plateful for Leona who remained mesmerized by the stars. Even as she ate, she kept glancing up. It was only when a deep rumble sounded from somewhere in the dark that she came back down to earth. 'What was that?'

'Lion,' Jake said casually. He was quite used to hearing the deep throaty sound of lions calling out in the night and he bit his lip to stop himself from laughing out loud at the horrified expression on Leona's face.

'A lion!' she gasped, edging closer to the fire. 'Is it coming here?'

'I doubt it,' Rick told her. 'He's miles away.'

Leona relaxed but jumped when another sound pierced the night. *Whoop, whoop*. It sounded much closer than the lion's roar, as if the animal was right on the edge of the camp.

'What's *that*?' Leona's voice trembled and she shuffled even closer to the fire so that she was almost sitting in it.

'Hyenas,' Jake told her. 'And they won't come into camp either.'

'But they're so close,' she protested.

'Perhaps not,' said Morgan. 'Sound travels a long way at night.'

'Yes. All of a few metres,' Jake teased.

Morgan shook his head. 'Don't listen to him, Leona. Those hyenas aren't anywhere near here. You're quite safe.'

After dinner, Jake went to take his shower. He fetched his towel and a cake of soap from the tent that he was sharing with Rick, then went to the kitchen fire and scooped a bucketful of hot water out of the deep three-legged pot. 'Thanks for this,' he said to Jackson who, with his assistant, had drawn the water from the river earlier that day.

With the water slopping over the sides of the bucket, Jake walked back through the camp on his way to the makeshift shower. The others were leaning back on their cushions again, enjoying coffee and chocolate around the fire.

'Enjoy your shower,' Leona said as Jake walked past her.

'And mind you don't make the floor too soggy,' joked Mr Samsudin, who had just come back from the primitive shower himself.

'I'll do my best,' Jake said.

Leaving the softly lit camp, Jake was soon surrounded by solid darkness. 'I should have brought my torch,' he muttered. But he didn't feel like going back for it. Crickets chirped in the bushes on either side of the narrow path and bats swooped in front of him as he made his way towards the shower area.

Before long, his eyes adjusted to the darkness and he was able to see the clearing just ahead of him. 'That's better,' he told himself.

When he got there, he draped his towel over a bush, kicked off his shoes, then poured the hot water into the shower bucket and hoisted it up into the air. Glancing round to make sure he was alone, he quickly stripped before reaching up and opening the tap in the bucket.

'This is great,' he chuckled, standing under the jet of hot water and soaping himself all over.

But Jake's was not the only laughter that penetrated the still dark night. Just then, loud, rude chortles came from beyond the clearing, as if someone had spied on Jake and was doubled-up at the sight of him stripped to his birthday suit in the middle of the bush.

Whoo, hoo, hoo, hoop, whoop! Whoop-whoop!

'Get lost!' Jake called out, realizing that it was a pack of hyenas.

But instead of fading, the hyenas' whooping laughter seemed to be coming closer.

Whoop-whoop. Hoo.

Jake peered towards the dense bushes from where the shrill cackles were coming. His heart lurched. Staring straight back at him were several pairs of bright yellow eyes, hovering above the ground as if disembodied by the pitch dark.

'Yikes!' he gasped.

Hoop-hoo-whoop-whoop-whoop.

Jake couldn't stand it any longer. Grabbing his towel, he sprinted barefoot down the path, leaving water pouring out of the bucket and his clothes lying in a heap on the ground.

Behind him, the hyenas whooped and hollered like a gang of hooligans.

Clutching the towel around his middle, Jake dashed into the centre of the camp then skidded to a halt and tried to look casual as he made his way towards his tent.

But there was no way of keeping the nerve-wracking experience to himself. Everyone must have heard the hyenas too, because they were all looking towards the path and had seen Jake's breathless arrival.

'What's the matter?' Leona called out. 'Hyenas all of a few metres away? They won't come into camp.' She mockingly repeated Jake's words to her. And with that came a blinding flash as she raised her camera and took a snapshot of the shell-shocked Jake draped in only a towel.

FIVE

'You should have seen his face, Shani!' laughed Leona. 'He looked as if he'd seen a ghost.'

'That's because you blinded me with the flash,' Jake defended himself. 'I wasn't scared at all.'

It was early evening, two days later. Jake and the rest of the hiking party had arrived back at the Bermans' house half an hour earlier at the end of their thrilling wilderness experience. It was very hot, so Jake, Shani and Leona had met up at the pool for a swim before dinner.

Shani wanted to hear all about the trail, but before Jake could tell her anything really interesting, Leona butted in with her version of the hyena incident at the camp shower.

'If you weren't scared, why did you run away from the hyenas?' she teased, dangling her legs in the water.

'Probably because Jake knows that all wild animals are unpredictable,' Shani suggested fairly. She was sitting waist-deep in the water on the top step.

Jake was about to dive into the deep end, but he paused and nodded. 'Exactly.' Thank goodness there was at least one sensible person around!

'That's not the impression you gave me,' ribbed Leona. 'I mean you *predicted* that they wouldn't come into camp.'

'Come off it, Leona,' Jake said irritably. 'Those hyenas *didn't* come into camp. They just got quite close, that's all. They're scavengers, you know. They'd probably smelled our supper and were on the scrounge for leftovers.' He dived into the cool water and when he surfaced, he looked at Leona and said, 'I've just realized. Those hyenas probably *did* come into camp after we'd all gone to bed. I bet they were nosing about for hours looking for scraps of food. You're lucky you didn't get up in the night to go to the loo. We might never have seen you again.'

Leona's jaw dropped. 'Really?'

'Uh-huh. I've even heard of hyenas dragging people out of their tents,' Jake went on, sounding deadly serious.

'Stop it, Jake.' Shani sounded like a cross parent. 'He's only teasing you, Leona. That kind of thing hardly ever happens.'

'Hardly ever?' Leona echoed, still looking rather horrified. 'So that means sometimes hyenas *do* take people!'

'Only once in a blue moon,' Jake said, thinking he'd better tone things down a bit. After all, Leona was a guest and he shouldn't really be teasing her, even if she'd started it. She'd probably had enough scares over the last few days to last her a lifetime. Just this afternoon, on the way back to the house, a big male warthog had shot out of a disused antbear hole just metres in front of them. Leona had nearly passed out! For about an hour afterwards, she was so keyed-up that even the tiniest rustle made her jump. 'You probably find it's only when people do something really stupid that hyenas go for them,' Jake finished.

'What sort of things?' Leona persisted, as if she was afraid she might have done something stupid herself.

'I don't know. Like leaving their tents open at night. Or,' Jake grinned, 'taking a solo shower in the bush.'

Jake's quip relaxed Leona. She laughed then slipped into the water and swam to the shallow end. 'By the way,' she said, floating on to the top step next to Shani, 'were there any calls for me while we were on the trail?'

Shani frowned. 'I don't think so. Were you expecting any?'

'Maybe. It's just that Lawrence tried to phone me on my mobile but my dad cut him off. I thought that perhaps he'd try the land line.'

'Who's Lawrence?' asked Shani.

'My boyfriend.'

Shani's eyes grew wide. 'You have a boyfriend?'

'Uh-huh. He's lovely.' Leona's face took on a

dreamy expression. 'Do you want to see a photograph of him?'

'Sure,' said Shani eagerly.

Leona stood up and wrapped a sarong around herself. 'I've got some pictures in my room. Come on. I'll show them to you.'

'OK. Cool!' said Shani, grabbing her towel.

'Don't forget the other photos we're supposed to look at,' Jake reminded them. 'The ones my mum said she'd show everyone.'

Hannah was a freelance wildlife photographer. The businessmen had heard about her work and had asked if they could see some of it, so Hannah was putting on a small display that evening.

'We'll look at them later,' Shani called back.

Jake swam a few more lengths before going into the house to change. He pulled on clean shorts and a T-shirt, then went out to the back patio where they were going to have a barbeque to celebrate the success of the first wilderness trail. Jake was in charge of cooking the meat. Since coming to live in Musabi, he'd become a bit of a barbeque expert, so Rick always assigned him to the job whenever they were catering for guests. Jake didn't mind. It wasn't a bad way of earning pocket money, and it definitely beat pulling out noxious weeds!

He struck a match and lit the coals under the grate of the built-in brick barbeque. He expected Shani and Leona to pitch up at any moment, but there was no sign of them. *How long does it take to look at a photo of some guy*? he wondered.

There was a bottle of Coke standing in a bucket of ice beside the barbecue along with some beers. He poured himself a glass of Coke and took a handful of peanuts from a bowl on the buffet table. Then, alternately sipping his drink and popping the nuts into his mouth, he looked at his mum's photographs that had been framed and put up on a wooden trellis next to the patio. Rick had even rigged up a spotlight so they could be seen in the dark.

There were about thirty pictures, all of them enlargements of shots Hannah had taken during the two years that she'd lived in Musabi. Many of the photographs were of birds, animals and weird-looking insects inside the reserve, but some had been taken in other areas, like the chimpanzee sanctuary in Uganda that Jake and Hannah had visited a while back.

'Superb pictures,' came a voice behind Jake. It was Mr Samsudin. Hannah and the two other businessmen were with him.

'Yeah. Mum's a brilliant photographer,' Jake agreed proudly.

Hannah smiled. 'Thanks for the vote of confidence.'

'It's a pity you weren't on the trail with us,' said Mr Cheng. 'There were some incredible photo opportunities.'

'So Rick told me. But surely you had cameras with you?'

'Yes. Leona had a still camera,' said Mr Lin. 'And Henry had a video camera – we're planning to make a short promotional video to market our lodge.'

'But I'm an amateur. I don't think my footage will be anything nearly as good as your pictures,' Mr Cheng said modestly.

Mr Samsudin was studying a close-up of a white rhino which had the longest horns Jake had ever seen. 'Perhaps you would let us buy some prints to put in our brochures? Like this one of the rhino, for instance. If people get a taste of the formidable beasts that inhabit this area, they'll want to come here in their droves.'

Oh no, Jake groaned to himself. *A few more tourists might be OK. But not* droves *of them.* Hearing soft laughter, he looked over his shoulder. Shani and Leona had appeared and were whispering to each other.

'What took you two so long?' Jake asked.

'Nothing,' said Shani who had changed from her swimsuit into a short, flowered skirt and a strappy red top, an outfit Jake guessed belonged to Leona who was similarly dressed. 'We were just trying out some of Leona's make-up, and the perfume she bought on the plane,' Shani continued.

As she came closer to him, Jake noticed that Shani was wearing lipstick. This was definitely a first for her and it made her look a lot older than her twelve years. Jake also caught a powerful whiff of perfume.

It stuck in his throat and made him cough. 'That's strong stuff,' he said when he'd stopped coughing. He waved his hand in front of his face, trying to chase away the scent.

'It's a lot better than rhino dung,' said Shani, sounding miffed. Leona must have told her about the way Jake, Rick and Morgan had handled the dung.

'That's your opinion,' Jake retorted, but added with a grin, 'I think I'd go for the dung any day.'

'How divine!' breathed Leona.

Divine! Rhino dung? was Jake's instant, and very surprised, reaction. But then he saw that Leona was looking at a close-up of a young chimpanzee.

'Would you just look at this?' she sighed.

'That's Ashai. Jake helped to rescue her in Uganda,' Hannah explained, going to stand next to Leona.

'She's the cutest thing!' Leona looked at the little chimp's wrinkled face and sad expression. 'Almost like a human baby.'

Jake waited for her to say she'd love to have a baby chimp as a pet. *I'll soon put her straight*! he thought. Ashai was a perfect example of why people shouldn't have chimps – or any wild animal for that matter – as pets.

Ashai's story was a tragic one. Along with the other adults in the chimp troop, her mother had been butchered by poachers to be sold as illegal bushmeat. Ashai, who was about three years old, had escaped into the nearby bushes where Jake had found her; the rest of the orphaned babies had been taken for sale on the black market as pets. But thanks to Jake and his friend Ross, whose parents ran the chimp sanctuary, the hunters had been arrested and the chimps united with another troop in the sanctuary. Still, this could never make up for the terrible loss they'd suffered. And as long as the illegal trade in chimps continued, it wouldn't be the last time chimpanzees were victims of such brutality.

Fully expecting Leona to ask her dad to buy her a chimp, Jake was relieved when she merely asked, 'Why did you have to rescue her, Jake? Was she stolen or something?'

'*She* wasn't. But others were.' Jake went on to tell Leona the full story.

'That sort of thing happens in the Far East too,' said Leona when Jake had finished.

Mr Lin nodded sombrely. 'Leona's right. We sometimes hear of rare apes and monkeys being smuggled out to other countries, and ending up in private zoos or research centres.'

'Pity there aren't more heroes like you and Ross to rescue them,' said Leona.

'But there *are* organizations that do many things to save the apes,' put in Mr Lin. 'Like the Born Free Foundation, which is based in the UK.'

'Yes, they do some fantastic work,' Hannah agreed.

'And anyway, I don't think we *were* heroes,' Jake

replied modestly, although he couldn't help feeling chuffed by Leona's reaction. 'We just did what we could.'

Leona was adamant. 'That's called being a hero.'

'Superjake!' Shani teased and ducked as Jake flicked a peanut at her.

When the visitors had seen all the photographs, they sat down round the fire while Shani went to help Hannah add the dressings to the salads. Jake fetched the meat from the kitchen and when he came back, he saw that Rick had arrived. He'd been to see that the staff and donkey team had returned safely from Nyika.

'Beer?' Rick offered the three businessmen.

'Yes, please,' said Leona.

Her father glared at her so that she quickly said, 'I'm only teasing.'

Jake raised his eyebrows disbelievingly. Leona thought she was so grown-up, she'd probably drink a beer, or at least a glass of wine, just to try and prove how sophisticated she was.

Jake flipped a few pieces of steak over, then put some sausages on the fire. They sizzled in the heat, giving off a spicy aroma.

'Mmm, smells good,' said Mr Samsudin.

Mr Lin was reclining in a deck chair. He took the beer Rick gave him and sighed contentedly. 'It has been a most wonderful three days. I have enjoyed myself enormously.'

'Even the shower?' Rick grinned.

Mr Lin hadn't been particularly impressed by the camp shower. He'd struggled to carry the bucket of water up the path and Morgan had gone to help him. Then he'd come back saying that he'd had trouble keeping his feet clean in the soggy ground. Jake knew what he meant. It was quite a mission to stand in the mud on one foot while drying the other. It also meant that while one foot might have been clean and dry, the other was always going to be a bit muddy! So on both nights that they were in the camp, Jake had fetched Mr Lin some hot water from the kitchen fire at bedtime so that he could wash his feet again before he got into his sleeping bag.

'Oh, the shower wasn't too bad,' said Mr Lin. 'In fact, it was quite an experience to stand out in the open under a bucket of water! Still,' he went on, his brown eyes good-humoured behind his spectacles, 'I think we will go for more, shall we say, normal showers in our lodge! With a few mod cons for comfort.'

'You mean, they'll have gold-plated taps and all that?' chuckled Leona.

'Perhaps not quite that lavish,' replied Mr Lin. 'Going by the plans, they'll be practical but smart – and indoors!'

'So the plans for your lodge are drawn up already?' asked Rick, looking interested.

'Oh, yes,' said Mr Cheng. 'We brought them with us. Would you like to see them?'

'Well, if you don't mind,' said Rick.

Mr Cheng turned to Leona who was staring up at the night sky, as spellbound as ever. 'Would you fetch the plans from the chalet please, Leona? They're on the coffee table in the sitting room.'

Leona raised her eyebrows. 'You want me to go to the chalets in the dark, alone? What if there's something out there?'

'There won't be. But if you like, I'll get them,' Jake offered.

'Thanks, Jake. You see, you *are* a hero,' Leona chuckled.

Jake made a face at her as he handed the barbeque tongs to Rick. 'Don't let the meat burn,' he warned his stepdad, then went through the house and across the front lawn to the guest quarters. He pushed open the door to the Chengs' chalet and switched on the light, disturbing a bushbaby that had slipped through an open window and was plundering a bowl of fruit on the coffee table. The fluffy-tailed creature stared at him with enormous, startled eyes then leaped on to the back of a chair and from there to the window sill. It sat there for a moment, looking regretfully at the fruit before sliding sideways through the narrow opening and disappearing into the night.

He'll be back as soon as I've gone, Jake thought. He knew he should close the window, but couldn't bring himself to.

There were two files on the coffee table, both labelled *Safari World*. One file was marked *Phase 1* and the other, *Phase 2*.

Jake opened the file for Phase 1. Several sheets of plans were neatly folded inside. He unfolded the top sheet and saw an artist's impression of a sprawling multi-storeyed building. 'It's *huge*!' he gasped out loud, his worst fears confirmed. 'There must be rooms for hundreds of people.'

And if that was just Phase 1, what would Phase 2 look like? Jake opened the second file. What he saw left him totally flabbergasted. This was far worse than anything he could have ever imagined. Dotted across a map of East Africa were about a dozen bright red labels all marked *Safari World*. There were five in Tanzania alone, with the rest across the borders in Kenya, Uganda and Malawi.

'They're going to develop a whole chain of *Safari Worlds*!' Jake exclaimed. He thumped the table. 'They can't do that. There'll be millions of people everywhere! They'll be like the lantana, taking over the wilderness and ruining everything.'

SIX

'It's like an African theme park – in Africa!' Jake told Hannah. He'd bumped into her in the house on his way back to the patio with the plans. 'And bigger than any theme park you've ever seen.'

'You're exaggerating, Jake,' his mum told him, going into the kitchen.

Jake followed her in. 'No, I'm not. Look here.' He glanced over his shoulder to make sure no one was coming, then opened the second file and showed it to Hannah. 'See what I mean?'

Hannah glanced at the plan as she bent down to take some freshly baked bread out of the oven, then did a rapid double-take. 'Oh my, it's horrendous!' she exclaimed.

'Rick will flip his lid when he sees it,' Jake predicted darkly.

But out on the patio, Rick politely kept his cool when Mr Cheng unfolded the plans with a flourish. 'It's going to be a very costly project,' was all he said, although he exchanged a fleeting look with Hannah and Jake that betrayed just how appalled he was.

Mr Lin mentioned a staggering sum of money that he and his colleagues, as well as some other financiers, were putting up for the project. 'But we'll reap good returns on our investment very quickly,' he explained. 'People are starting to see Africa as one of the most exciting holiday playgrounds on earth.'

Holiday playground! Jake thought with disgust. *The wilderness isn't a playground. Nor should it be part of some giant theme park. It's home to animals that have been here for millions of years and should be left alone.*

For the rest of the evening, Jake found it impossible to join in the conversation. All he could think of was the *Safari World* chain. The more he thought about it, the more he saw it as an evil giant weed, reaching its long, greedy shoots deep into the bush and taking over the animals' habitat.

Next morning, the three businessmen drove off in their hired jeep. They hoped to start negotiations with local chiefs to acquire the land for the first phase of their development. Leona stayed behind, preferring to spend the day lazing next to the pool.

'They *can't* do it,' Jake protested to his mum and Rick as they watched the Land Rover drive away. 'We have to stop them.'

'I don't think we can,' sighed Rick.

'Can't we warn the chiefs? Tell them exactly what *Safari World* will do?' Jake urged.

Hannah put a hand on Jake's shoulder. 'You might find they'll see the development in a completely different way, as a means of generating jobs for local people. You know how badly that is needed.'

Jake understood what his mum meant. In the rural areas there was almost no work, and life was often very tough for the people who lived there. Anything that could provide them with jobs was usually very welcome. One example was the elephant-proof fence that Rick had put up along one of the boundaries of Musabi before bringing in a herd of elephants from Zambia. Dozens of locals had worked on the fence. But it had been only a temporary job and when it was finished, so too were the wages.

'People need permanent employment,' Hannah continued. 'And it wouldn't be fair to expect them not to jump at the opportunities that come their way.'

'It'll change everything,' Jake complained. 'For the worse.' He could see Leona over at the pool. She was lying in the sun, listening to her personal stereo. Jake was about to follow Rick and Hannah indoors when he saw Shani arriving at the swimming pool. She'd finished her chores early and had changed from her everyday shorts and T-shirt into a fashionable, bright pink sarong which probably belonged to Leona.

Jake watched as Shani placed her towel on the paving next to Leona who sat up and offered her one of the earphones for the stereo. Moments later, the two new friends were sunbathing side by side, their feet tapping in time to the music.

That's just the sort of thing I mean, Jake thought. He couldn't help thinking how she had changed in the short time she'd known Leona. Only a day or two ago, Shani wasn't the least interested in make-up and perfume and the latest fashion. *And now that's all she can think about. She doesn't even want to come on the trail tomorrow.*

The second trail was starting the very next day and, after all the excitement of the first one, Jake could hardly wait. This time there were going to be only two tourists, the Achesons, a married couple from England who had read about the Wilderness Trail on the Musabi website. They were due to arrive later that afternoon.

At first, Shani had been keen to go too, especially when she'd heard about Pea. But after last evening, when she and Leona had talked nonstop – 'girl talk', Jake assumed – she'd suddenly changed her mind and opted instead to keep Leona company.

She's welcome, Jake thought grumpily, bending down to pat Bina who was licking his ankle. He couldn't think of anything more boring than lying in the sun listening to music, or sitting inside trying on face paint! Especially when across the fence lay the most exciting place in the world.

* * *

It was a very small group that set out on the trail early the following morning – just Jake, Morgan, and Gavin and Jo Acheson. Rick had been called away to an urgent meeting of conservationists at the nearby Rungwa Wildlife Sanctuary, but he was confident that, with only two guests on the trail, Morgan could handle things without him. Also, Jake was there to help out. Hannah would have gone on the trail too, but with some of the rangers busy with a game count and others on foot patrol in various parts of Musabi, this would have meant leaving the office unattended until Rick returned.

'Jake, you're the rearguard this time. Whistle if you see any danger,' said Morgan as they started out from the house in the soft red light of dawn.

'Shouldn't I have a gun?' Jake chanced at asking.

'Forget it,' Morgan said sternly, even though it was obvious Jake wasn't being serious. 'The first time you handle a gun is when you're sixteen. And then, like your dad says, it'll only be a pellet gun.'

'I hope you're good at whistling,' said Jo Acheson with a grin.

The Achesons were a young professional couple from London; he was a lawyer and his wife a company director. When he'd first set eyes on them yesterday afternoon, he thought they were the last people who should be going on the hike. They were ultra glamorous and real city types – a lot like Leona, really. They'd come to do the trail to celebrate their wedding anniversary. But, during drinks on the patio later in the evening, it became clear that the Achesons were prepared to take on whatever challenges the bush held in store.

'Just as long as I don't have to burrow underground at bed time,' Jo had laughed when Morgan was giving them the lowdown on the trail. 'I'm not too good at digging.' She'd held up her immaculately manicured hands.

'How are you at fetching buckets of water for your shower?' Jake couldn't resist pitching in.

'She's a past master,' Gavin had answered for Jo. 'She has her own packhorse. Me!'

The four hikers went through the gate in the fence and almost immediately had to move aside to let the real pack animals, the donkeys, go past. They were later than usual this morning because two of the donkeys had managed to get out of their enclosure in the night. The handlers discovered this just before dawn and spent a difficult half hour looking for the pair that had gone AWOL.

'Lucky no lions got them,' Jake remarked as the donkeys went past, their hooves clopping over the stony ground.

'Then I *would* have been a packhorse,' said Gavin. He raised his hand to greet the handlers. '*Jambo habari*.'

'You speak Swahili!' Jake said, impressed. He'd picked up some of the local language himself, mainly thanks to Shani, but this had taken him months. Yet here was a guest, newly arrived from London, trotting out a greeting as if he was fluent in the language.

Jo immediately put Jake right. 'No, he doesn't. He's just repeating something he learned by heart from a phrase book he bought at Heathrow.'

One of the donkey handlers started to speak rapidly to Gavin in Swahili and the visitor was instantly at a complete loss. He stared at the man, then turned to Morgan and said, 'Er, could you translate for me, please?'

'Sure. He's greeting you in return. He says that all is well with him and his family and his cattle. And he asks if it is the same with your family and everyone in your country.' Morgan grinned. 'And the Queen of England too.'

Gavin laughed. 'In that case, please tell him that all of England, including the Queen and her family, were very well the last time I checked.'

'That's a fabulous way of greeting people,' said Jo as the donkey team went past, before veering off the path and continuing in a direct line down into the valley. 'I think I'll take that idea back to London with me.'

That'll make a change, Jake thought, grinning at the tall, blonde-haired young woman. *Someone taking an idea away, rather than bringing a whole bunch of strange ideas in.*

This morning's route was a different one to that they'd taken on the first trail. Morgan followed the game path for a few hundred metres then joined another that led to a waterhole. 'We might be lucky enough to see a few animals coming down to drink,' he said.

The path took them across an open plain, then through a forested area and across a narrow stream. On the way, they encountered small herds of impala, a pair of stately-looking waterbuck, and a family of rock hyraxes sunning themselves on an outcrop of rocks. Jo and Gavin were delighted with each new sighting, recording everything on their expensive digital cameras.

'You haven't seen anything yet,' Jake chuckled when they paused to watch a troop of monkeys foraging in a fig tree. 'Just wait until we come across black rhinos again.' He was sure they would, as soon as they came to a tamboti forest.

Eventually, through a grove of trees, Jake spotted what looked more like a swamp than a drinking hole. Dense clumps of papyrus reeds grew in the water and a tall green-barked fever tree towered over the clearing. Apart from a few small brown birds pecking in the churned-up mud flats, and the masked weavers busily building their nests in the fever tree, the place looked deserted.

Cautiously, they approached the marsh. From somewhere nearby came a shushing, rustling noise, a few low grunts, then a quickly fading pattering sound, like feet or hooves skipping across the ground.

'Sounds like we disturbed something,' whispered Gavin.

Morgan nodded. 'Probably warthogs wallowing in the mud. But just about anything could be lurking here. Let's stop for a while and see.'

The four of them waited in silence behind a clump of bushes for what, to Jake, seemed like ages. Allergic to sitting still when there was nothing to see, he quickly grew restless, especially when a line of ants began climbing up his leg. 'There's nothing here. Let's go,' he whispered to Morgan, brushing the ants on to the ground. Momentarily disorientated, the ants swarmed around in confused circles until they found their bearings, then started up Jake's leg again.

'*Saburi!*' Morgan said under his breath. 'Patience is always rewarded.'

'How? With ants treating you like a motorway?' Jake whispered back. He flicked the ants away again.

Jo was sitting next to Gavin on a low flat rock, watching the industrious weavers through her binoculars. The handsome black-and-yellow male birds flew back and forth, gathering strips of reeds which they then wove into their nests under the critical gaze of the duller-coloured females. 'Isn't is peaceful here?' Jo remarked, lowering her binoculars.

Jake yawned. 'Too peaceful.'

'Peaceful enough for me to nip behind a bush for a minute?' asked Gavin.

'OK. But be careful,' Morgan replied.

Gavin eased off his backpack and left it on the ground, then, glancing round, he slipped away into a thicket a little way off. He was out of sight for only a fraction of a second before he came dashing back, shock written all over his face. 'Come quickly,' he puffed to Morgan.

Jake scrambled to his feet. 'What is it?'

But Gavin was already sprinting back through the thicket, beckoning urgently to the others.

Throwing all caution to the wind, Jake, Morgan and Jo ran after him. Jake figured that whatever was behind those bushes couldn't have been all that dangerous otherwise Gavin wouldn't be in such a hurry to get back to it.

Rounding the thicket, Jake felt his breath knocked out of him. Lying motionless on its side on the ground, just metres away, was a huge black rhino.

For a brief horrible moment Jake thought it was Nina, but felt a jolt of relief when he saw no sign of Pea. Then his eyes fell on the cruel wire noose that bit tightly into the animal's neck, in places disappearing right into the wrinkled grey skin. Another length of wire gripped one front foot. Both nooses were on running loops attached to a thick wire that was stretched between two trees, right across the rhino's path. The poor creature hadn't stood a chance. Once caught in the hideous trap, it would have struggled as hard as it could. And with each desperate movement, the nooses would have been pulled ever tighter, slicing into its neck until the last breath was choked from it.

And as if that wasn't enough, the reason for this magnificent animal's terrible death was starkly obvious, making Jake feel sick to his stomach. Where the rhino's lower horn should have been, was now just a jagged, bony base.

SEVEN

'How dare they!' Jake burst out. Every fibre in his body was filled with pure hatred for the poachers who had done this. He ran forward, determined to do something, anything.

Morgan grabbed his shoulder and stopped him. 'There's nothing you can do, Jake.'

'There is!' Jake argued. 'We can pick up the poachers' trail and follow them.'

'That's too dangerous,' said Morgan. 'We don't know how many there are. And they'll be well armed.'

'I don't care,' insisted Jake. 'We *have* to find them.' He shrugged off Morgan's firm grip and dashed over to the slain rhino, hot tears coursing down his cheeks. In his mind, he heard again Rick's words from just a few days ago. *The six have become seven*. 'And now they're six again!' he said with feeling.

Gavin and Morgan followed him, leaving Jo at the edge of the clearing with her head bowed. For a moment, the three of them stood silently side by side, staring at the pitiful sight.

'Poor fellow,' Gavin murmured after a while. 'It looks like he put up a terrible fight.'

The snares had cut deeply into the rhino's leg and neck, exposing the tender flesh beneath the thick grey hide. Bloated blue flies swarmed around the open wounds, feeding on the dried blood that crusted the rhino's skin.

'It was a fight he couldn't win,' Jake said angrily, pointing to a small round bullet hole between the rhino's eyes. 'And to think that he came to Musabi to be safe!' he added miserably.

Morgan sighed. 'Unfortunately, nowhere is safe from poachers. As long as there's value in things like rhino horn and ivory, unscrupulous people will go to any length to get it.'

On the other side of the clearing, Jo let out a stifled sob. 'How can anyone be so greedy?' she wondered out loud, her voice choked with emotion.

Jake glanced at her and nodded in agreement, then stared down at the rhino again. He could hardly tear his eyes away from the stubby remains of the animal's lower horn. He wondered briefly why the poachers had only hacked off that one. Perhaps the upper horn, which was quite small, was less valuable to them than the bigger, bottom one. *Or we disturbed them before they could take it. Which means they could try their luck again. They might even have a go at the rest of the rhinos!*

Jake went cold. 'We've got to find the poachers!'

he insisted again. He studied the dusty ground, hoping to find footprints they could follow. But all he could see were some marks that looked as if the poachers had used branches to sweep the ground to cover their tracks. 'There has to be *some* trace of them,' he muttered to himself.

'Forget it, Jake,' said Morgan sternly. 'We're not following any trail. We'll leave that to the game guards.'

'That could be too late.' Something shiny glinted at Jake from a clump of grass. He bent down and picked it up. 'It's an empty cartridge! Here's some evidence,' he said to the others.

Gavin took the cartridge and rolled it around in his hand. 'I guess we should hang on to it in case it helps to identify the criminals. But unless they're rounded up, this isn't worth much.' He sounded as if he knew what he was talking about and Jake remembered that he was a lawyer.

'We'll round them up all right,' Jake promised. He was more furious than he could remember being in a long time. *This is never going to happen in Musabi again,* he vowed silently. It was the second time since Jake had come to live there that poachers had preyed on newly relocated animals. Soon after Rosa and her elephant herd had come from Zambia, he and Shani had helped foil a poaching attempt. The poachers were strangers pretending to be working on the elephant-proof fence. It was sheer luck that one of them had dropped a mobile phone; Jake and Shani had found out what the men were really up to when they returned the phone to them.

'We'd better get back and break the bad news to Rick,' said Morgan, breaking into Jake's thoughts. 'The sooner the guards are sent out, the better.' He looked at Gavin and Jo. 'I'm sorry I have to cut short your hike in the wilderness.'

'Don't apologize,' said Jo at once. 'I couldn't live with myself if we just continued on our way.'

'And we can always come back another time,' added Gavin.

Before they left the clearing, with the sorry heap of rhino in its centre, Jake scouted around on either side of the game path hoping to find some last-minute evidence that could be useful in identifying the poachers. He was about to give up when he spotted a single footprint in a patch of sandy soil next to a bush. He looked closer and saw several other prints. They were leading away from the game path, in the opposite direction to the waterhole, but disappeared in the long grass beyond the patch of sand. Still, Jake was able to make out three distinct patterns from the undersoles of boots.

'Look. There were three poachers,' he called. 'And they went this way.' An overwhelming urgency gripped him. 'Come on, Morgan. We have to go after them now. I bet it was them we heard running away when we got to the waterhole.'

'What makes you think that?' asked Jo.

'It's just a hunch,' said Jake. 'But if you think about it, it's just too much of a coincidence. How many animals have we heard galloping away from us this morning?' Before anyone could respond he gave the answer himself. 'None!' He made a final appeal to Morgan. 'Look, they probably wouldn't have covered up their tracks the whole way. And they're probably not even that far away yet.'

But Morgan shook his head. 'No. I'm responsible for the three of you, and I'm not prepared to risk anyone's safety going after a gang of armed men.' He slung his rifle over his shoulder. 'We'll leave it to the proper authorities.'

Gavin must have seen the look of frustration on Jake's face. 'Morgan's right, you know. As he said, the gang is probably armed to the teeth, while we have only one rifle between us,' he said reasonably.

Jake shrugged. He knew now that no amount of persuading would see him get his way. But there was one thing he felt they ought to do before they left the rhino to the vultures. He grabbed the wire that was strung between the two trees. 'Let's at least do something about this death trap.'

'Not a bad idea,' said Gavin. 'That way the poachers won't be able to use it again.' He took a stainless steel gadget that looked like a penknife out of his pocket. 'Let's see if this is as good as the advert promised.' He opened it up and unfolded an impressive assortment of small tools.

'Let's see. Where is it?' muttered Gavin, sorting through a bottle opener, a screwdriver, a file, a tin opener, a pair of pliers, a knife, and finally, some wire-cutters. 'Ah, here they are.'

Morgan looked doubtfully at the small tool. 'Do you think they'll cut that thick wire?'

'It's worth a try.' Gavin began to clip at the wire close to one tree, sawing the cutters to and fro to help them bite down on the metal strand. In no time at all he'd cut right through it, then he made a start on the other end.

'Not bad,' said Morgan.

Soon, the wire snapped away from the second tree. Jake helped Gavin to pull it out of the running loops, then Morgan coiled it up and shoved it into his backpack. 'Right, let's go,' he said.

They started back the way they'd come, each of them glancing back at the unfortunate rhino one last time.

'We'll find the criminals who did this to you,' Jake promised softly when he paused to look back.

Jo was just in front of him. 'Yes. What goes around, comes around,' she said grimly.

Just then, Jake heard a low sound. *Hrrmph*. It was coming from a clump of tall bushes a little way ahead of them.

Hrrmph.

The others had heard the soft snorting sound too. They stopped and listened.

Hrrmph, hrrmph. There was no mistaking it.

'Rhino,' whispered Jake, instinctively looking round for the nearest tree. And as he did, he saw a huge black rhino standing half-hidden behind the bushes, his ears turning like miniature radar dishes as he tried to pinpoint the intruders.

'Don't move!' ordered Morgan as the rhino stamped the ground and snorted again.

The rhino peered short-sightedly toward them, sniffing the air while he kept on flicking his ears back and forth. He turned his head to the side to taste the air and Jake now saw just how long his lower horn was. *A poacher's dream*, Jake had just enough time to think before the rhino pawed the ground once more before charging forward with a dizzying burst of speed.

'Take cover!' shouted Morgan.

Quick as lightning, Gavin grabbed Jo's arm and pulled her to the nearest tree. He gave her a leg up, then climbed up after her, while Jake and Morgan ducked behind a disused ant-heap.

The rhino ran straight past them, his head held high. When he came to the clearing where the dead rhino lay, he skidded to a halt. *Hrmph!* he grunted, and, just as the three humans had done earlier, he stared silently at the fly-covered corpse.

Jake's throat tightened with emotion. What was going through the rhino's mind? Did he recognize the dead animal? Did he feel fear, or pity, or anger? He had heard of elephants grieving for dead relatives, so there was no reason why rhinos couldn't feel sorrow and anguish, too.

For a few minutes, the rhino stood over the hunched grey shape. His huge head swayed slowly from side to side as if he was deep in thought, before he gave one last snort and trotted away into the bushes.

'Be on your guard, *faru*,' murmured Morgan.

Jake frowned. '*Faru*?'

'Swahili for big rhino,' Morgan explained.

'Then that's what we'll call him,' Jake decided. He stood up and, peering over the top of the ant-heap, watched until he couldn't see Faru anymore.

'I don't think he meant to go for us at all when he charged,' Morgan remarked as he and Jake emerged from behind the anthill.

'What makes you say that?' asked Gavin, helping Jo down from the tree.

'Well, he went straight for the dead rhino, as if he had to see for himself what had happened,' replied Morgan.

Jake saw that Jo had dropped her sunglasses in her rush to get up the tree so he picked them up and handed them to her.

Jo polished the dark shiny lenses on her T-shirt. 'Do you think it will affect him?' she asked. 'Like make him angry with humans, or more protective of the other rhinos?'

'I don't know for sure,' Morgan admitted. 'But I

don't think we should hang around much longer. From the looks of it, that rhino understood exactly what had gone on here, which means he isn't going to take kindly to any more humans tramping around. If he feels threatened he could become very unpredictable, and that means the wilderness is not a safe place to be right now.' He rested his hand lightly on Jake's shoulder. 'Things aren't looking good, I know. But don't worry. One way or the other, we'll stop those three men from killing any more rhinos.'

'I hope you're right,' said Jake.

It took Rick and Morgan less than an hour to mobilize Musabi's four most skilled trackers. Arriving back at the house, Morgan had immediately jumped into a jeep and gone to fetch two men who were on foot patrol several kilometres away. Rick, who had only just returned from Rungwa, had radioed two other game guards who were supervising the construction of a new hide near a waterhole. He went white with anger when Morgan told him about the slaughtered rhino. Jake knew his stepdad felt as strongly as he did that Musabi should be a safe place for every animal, and especially those that were relocated from other areas that couldn't support them.

Gavin and Jo went to tell Hannah what had happened, while Jake was given the job of fetching the equipment the guards would need. He hurried to the storeroom at the back of the garages and took four walkie-talkie radios off the shelves, as well as a couple of lightweight tents in case the men would have to spend the night in the open. The poachers already had a good start on the trackers so they could be just about anywhere in the vast wilderness area.

Jake glanced at the aerial-like receiver that was used for tracking animals that were implanted with transmitters, and briefly wished there was a similar electronic way of finding the poachers. *They wouldn't stand a chance of getting away then*, he mused.

Back at the house, the four trackers had gathered on the veranda. Gavin and Jo were there too, in case the game guards needed some information from them. Morgan had driven to Sibiti, the nearest village, to take the Land Rover's spare wheel to the garage to have a puncture repaired. Rick wanted all the vehicles to be roadworthy in case they were needed to help catch the poachers. Morgan promised to keep an eye open in case the poachers had managed to leave Musabi and were somewhere on the road by now.

Jake wondered for a moment where Shani was. She'd be furious when she heard what happened. He glanced across to the pool, but Shani and Leona weren't there anymore. *They're probably painting their faces and trying on clothes in Leona's room again*, Jake thought gloomily.

Rick was giving the guards their orders. 'Herbert, you and Kwanza go down to Nyika and tell the camp staff what has happened. They can keep an eye out for the poachers. Then head for the waterhole and see if you can pick up the poachers' tracks from there. Baraka and Patrick, I want you to concentrate on the boundary of the wilderness area. Radio me if you see anything suspicious,' Rick instructed the men.

'I'm going too,' said Jake. After all, he knew exactly where the incident had happened.

'No, you're not,' Rick told him in a tone that warned Jake not to think about arguing. 'It's far too dangerous.'

Feeling frustrated, Jake watched the rangers walk swiftly across the garden, their rifles at their sides and walkie-talkie radios slung across their chests. In their backpacks, they carried the tents as well as food and water which Hannah had hastily put together for them.

Once the men had gone through the gate, Rick turned to Jo and Gavin. 'I know you were hoping to go on another trail soon, but I'm going to have to disappoint you. Nervous rhinos and armed poachers on the run are a lethal mix, so I'm cancelling all the wilderness trails for the time being.'

Gavin nodded understandingly. 'Please don't worry on our account.' He put an arm round Jo's shoulders. 'We'll be quite happy to celebrate our anniversary by exploring the rest of Musabi.'

'There are some maps of the reserve in my office if you'd like to plan your game drives,' Hannah offered.

'Thanks. And we'll definitely come back when the trails are up and running again,' said Jo.

'We'll hold you to that,' said Hannah. 'I'm going to phone the people booked on the next trail to tell them it's been postponed, then I'll whip up some refreshments for you all. You must be exhausted, and famished.'

Jake wasn't in the bit least tired, and he certainly wasn't hungry. He kept thinking of the poachers roaming somewhere in the wilderness, on the lookout for the rest of the black rhinos. What if Nina was next on their list? That meant Pea was at risk, too, on the brink of being orphaned, just like Goliath when poachers killed his mother.

As for Faru, Jake couldn't get the grieving rhino out of his mind. His extra-long horn made him even more of a target than the others. 'Have you told the police yet?' Jake asked Rick.

'That's my next job,' Rick told him.

Jake went with his stepdad to the office, a thatched rondavel near the back fence. 'I can't work out why we didn't hear any gun shots,' he remarked as they crossed the lawn.

'Perhaps the *shiftas* had a silencer fitted to their gun,' suggested Rick, using the local word for poacher-bandits. 'They might have got wind of the wilderness trails and realized they had to be extra cautious if they weren't to be heard.'

'If they know what's happening in Musabi, they could be locals living somewhere around here,' Jake said.

'Perhaps,' Rick replied. 'But I wouldn't bet on it.' He pushed open his office door and went inside where he picked up the phone and dialled a number.

Jake pulled himself up to sit on Rick's desk.

'Oh, hello. Inspector Mku, please,' Rick said as someone answered the phone. He was put through to the inspector and explained what had happened. 'I've sent my guards down to track the poachers,' he said. 'But I'd appreciate some back-up from your Game Protection Unit if possible.'

The inspector must have agreed at once to send out some of his men because Rick thanked him then hung up.

'What will happen to the poachers when they're caught?' Jake asked.

'A heavy fine and a long prison sentence.'

'It doesn't seem worth the risk,' Jake mused as they left the office.

Rick stopped and looked at him. 'You think so? Well, think again. Guess what a rhino horn can end up earning on the black market?'

Jake frowned. 'I know elephant ivory is worth a lot. But each tusk is huge and weighs a ton. I don't know about one rhino horn though. A hundred pounds? Or dollars, maybe?'

'Guess again,' said Rick. 'Don't forget, ivory is turned into things like ornaments and jewellery, but rhino horns are in great demand for medicinal purposes. The tiniest amounts are believed to have great powers. And yet it's no more than hair really.'

Jake was surprised. 'Hair?'

'Yep. Just a lot of hollow fibres called keratin that are loosely bonded together. And for one horn alone, people are prepared to pay tens of thousands of dollars.'

Jake's jaw dropped. 'Tens of thousands of dollars? Just for a single horn?' How much would Faru's long horn be worth? As much as a house, or even a plane? Suddenly the big rhino seemed in even greater danger than before.

EIGHT

Jake paced restlessly back and forth along the western fence. For the umpteenth time that morning, he raised his binoculars and peered into the wilderness area. There was *still* no sign of the guards. They'd been gone nearly twenty-four hours. Had the three *shiftas* given the rangers the slip and got miles away from Musabi already?

'We should have gone after them yesterday,' Jake muttered, lowering the binoculars.

He heard a splash and looked across to the pool. Shani had just dived in. She broke the surface and, seeing him looking in her direction, waved to him. 'Come and join us,' she called. Jake noticed that Leona was lying on a lounger at the edge of the pool, sunbathing and listening to her CDs as usual.

'No thanks.' For once, Jake didn't feel like hanging out with Shani – not that he thought she'd notice. Every spare minute she had, she spent with Leona. *She's becoming Leona's clone,* Jake thought. So much so, that instead of saving up for the ordinary transistor radio she'd seen in the Dar es Salaam store, Shani had now set her sights on a personal stereo exactly like Leona's!

But what was even more worrying was that Shani didn't seem all that upset by the rhino incident. 'It's pretty bad,' was all she said before changing the subject yesterday when Jake told her about the snaring. This was completely out of character for Shani who'd always been quick to jump to the animals' defence when man tried to interfere with nature. Only recently, she'd been dead against a King Cheetah cub being taken into captivity by a tribe of people living fifty kilometres away from Musabi.

But now Shani seemed to have other things on her mind. *Big city things,* Jake thought moodily. He sighed, then started back towards the office to see if any of the guards had radioed Rick yet.

The sound of gunfire stopped him dead in his tracks. Appalled, he spun round, trying to locate where it was coming from. A second volley of shots cracked the air. It seemed a long way off, but all the same, he was sure it was coming from the wilderness area.

Jake went cold. Was it a shoot-out between the guards and the poachers? Or was the target another rhino?

Another burst of gunfire rang out. It was more than Jake could stand. Vaguely aware that Shani and

Leona were calling to him, he sprinted towards the office. Rick *had* to investigate immediately. And Jake was going with him.

But the first person Jake saw as he charged across the garden was Mr Cheng who'd just pulled up in his hired Land Rover.

'You in a hurry or something?' Mr Cheng grinned as he hauled an overnight bag out of the back of the vehicle.

'Yes,' Jake puffed, not wanting to waste any time explaining things. He saw Rick emerge from his office and stride across the lawn towards him, a walkie-talkie radio in his hands.

Another burst of gunfire broke out.

Mr Cheng looked surprised. 'Who's shooting? And where?'

'Dunno,' said Jake. Out of the corner of his eye, he saw Shani and Leona coming across from the swimming pool. He hurried on to meet Rick, with Mr Cheng hard on his heels, and Leona and Shani right behind him.

'Someone's shooting,' Jake said breathlessly to Rick.

'I heard it,' Rick responded, his expression grim, then, voicing Jake's own worst fears, added, 'I think it's down in the wilderness area. It had better not be those poachers.'

'Poachers?' frowned Mr Cheng and before Rick or anyone else could go into details, Leona told her father what she'd heard about the poaching incident.

'Maybe there's a gun battle going on between the guards and the poachers,' she speculated.

Mr Cheng looked grave. 'This is terrible news. And not only for the rhinos. People aren't going to want to visit a place where people shoot at each other.'

'Musabi isn't dangerous,' Jake burst out, irritated that Mr Cheng should be less interested in the plight of the rhinos than in how people would feel. 'It's the poachers who are making it that way.'

Rick was talking into his radio. 'Base to game guards, come in. Over.'

The radio crackled and hissed but there was no reply.

'Base to game guards. Come in please. Urgent. Over.'

There was still no reply.

'Drat. They're probably out of range,' said Rick. He strode towards the fence. Jake and the others hurried after him.

'Come in, game guards,' Rick called over the radio.

No answer.

If Jake had any patience left over, it drained right out of him now. 'We're wasting time. We've got to go down right now and see what's going on. The rhinos are in danger.' He was aware of Mr Cheng saying how glad he was not to be hiking through the wilderness when suddenly a distant voice came over the radio.

'Ranger to base, do you read me? Over.'

'Reading you. We heard shooting. What's happening? Over,' Rick replied.

Jake held his breath, desperately hoping not to hear that another rhino had fallen victim to the *shiftas*.

'Warning shots,' came the guard's reply, then his voice was lost in a burst of static.

'I'm losing you, Herbert,' said Rick. 'Can you repeat that, please? Over.'

Jake glanced at Shani. She stood next to Leona, their arms linked. The two friends seemed to be holding their breath while they waited for the ranger to speak again.

At least Shani looks worried, Jake told himself.

The ranger's voice came back more strongly. 'Warning shots. To stop a rhino fight.'

Stop a rhino fight! The words hit Jake like a blast of icy air. Did that mean the rhinos felt so threatened they were attacking each other?

'Two male rhinos,' continued the game guard. His voice grew indistinct again so that Jake could only pick up snatches of what he was saying. 'Serious clash . . . one . . . gashed . . . right shoulder.'

Shani, Leona and Mr Cheng all breathed a sigh of relief. 'Thank goodness it's not poachers,' said Shani. 'Everything's OK. The rhinos are probably just fighting over their territory.'

Jake rounded on her. 'No it's not OK. You can't be sure they're defending their territories. They might be fighting because they feel nervous.' He appealed to Rick. 'Isn't there anything we can do?'

Rick shook his head sympathetically. 'I'm afraid not. But don't worry too much. Remember, black rhinos don't often get into fights. And they're unlikely to go the whole nine yards until one is killed. One of them will back off before long. If it hasn't done already.'

But Jake couldn't help feeling worried sick for the rhinos. Their whole lives had been suddenly turned upside down and it seemed as if they instinctively knew this. 'Ask if the guards have seen any of the others,' Jake pressed his stepdad. 'And if they're on the poachers' trail yet.'

The answer to both questions was negative. Jake's frustration grew to bursting point. 'We've got to do more to find the poachers,' he urged.

'We're doing all we can,' was all Rick said.

Going back across the garden, Mr Cheng questioned Rick about the poaching incident. 'You say the rhino was shot?'

'That's right,' Rick replied. 'After he'd been snared.'

Mr Cheng blinked. 'So how dangerous are things in the wilderness right now?'

'It's hard to tell,' Rick said. 'The poachers will more than likely be on edge, so they could be quite trigger happy. And any further shooting could make the rhinos very nervous. That's why I've cancelled the wilderness trails for now.'

'This is definitely not good,' said Mr Cheng. 'I suppose you can't guarantee that it won't happen again?'

Rick shook his head.

'In that case, I think my colleagues and I might have to rethink our lodge plans,' said Mr Cheng. 'They've hired a car each and are still negotiating with the authorities. Andrew's in Arusha and Dato said he was going to speak to a chief somewhere near Sibiti. But they'll be back later today.'

'What do you mean, rethink the plans?' Leona queried.

Her father paused, then with a grave expression on his face, he said, 'Perhaps we shouldn't let our guests go on the wilderness trails. It might be too dangerous. All we need is for someone to get hurt on a trail and for the word to get out. That'll be bad for business, and our lodge could end up being a, er, white elephant.'

'White elephant!' Leona laughed. 'Very appropriate!'

But Jake didn't find it amusing at all. He didn't mind if the lodge lost out, but what about Musabi? The reserve relied on income from tourists and Rick had had high hopes of the wilderness trails becoming a big hit. Now it looked like this wouldn't happen. The poaching was having even more far-reaching consequences than Jake had first imagined. The threat was not just to the herd of black rhinos, but the whole of Musabi.

* * *

A few hours later, Patrick and Baraka, two of the trackers that Rick had sent down to the boundary, returned.

'We saw no one. Also no snares and no tracks, *Bwana*,' Baraka told Rick when they arrived at his office door. 'Those *shiftas* must be very experienced men. I think they must have left Musabi.'

Jake, who'd tailed Rick everywhere in case news came through from the guards, felt crushed by disappointment. The poachers might not be in Musabi any more, but that didn't mean they wouldn't be back, setting more snares to trap the rhinos. *And what if Nina's caught*? Jake shuddered, his heart once again heavy at the thought of the mother rhino being killed and Pea being left an orphan.

More than ever, he wanted to see Nina and her calf again. He had to satisfy himself that they were both all right. 'We have to go down to the wilderness,' he told Rick. 'Today.'

'What for? You heard Baraka. The *shiftas* have probably gone. Anyway, the other guards are still there,' Rick said.

'Can't we just go and check on the rhinos?' Jake persisted.

Rick shook his head. 'Leave it to the rangers, Jake. I can't be in two places at once. And you,' he added, guiding Jake over to the door, 'have work to do too. The pool needs cleaning.'

Jake groaned. Cleaning the pool seemed like the most unimportant thing in the world right now.

'Go on, Jake. It'll take your mind off the rhinos.'

It didn't. Standing at the side of the pool and brushing down the walls, he could think of nothing but Nina and Pea.

The sound of a car engine helped him to snap out of his reverie. Without thinking, he let go of the long aluminium pole that held the stiff nylon brush. It sank to the bottom of the pool.

'Too bad!' Jake muttered mutinously.

The vehicle coming up the drive was the Achesons' hired jeep. A second vehicle was not far behind them and Jake saw that it was the Musabi Land Rover with Morgan at the wheel.

Leaving the pole at the bottom of the pool, Jake went to find out if Gavin and Jo had had a successful game drive.

'We had a pretty good time,' said Gavin.

'Pretty good? It was exceptional!' Jo corrected him. 'We saw a cheetah and her cub resting under a tree on a plain not far from here.'

'Well, we think it was her cub, only it had rather unusual markings,' said Gavin.

'You mean blotches like ink stains, and stripes going down its spine?' Jake asked, feeling a ripple of excitement.

Jo was intrigued. 'How on earth did you know?'

'That's Cheepard,' Jake said proudly, forgetting his

anxiety over the rhinos for a brief moment as he pictured the beautiful little cub that the tribe in the north had wanted to take into captivity. 'He's a King Cheetah and he's probably even more rare than the black rhino.'

'How lucky we were then,' said Jo. 'And talking of rhinos, any luck on the poacher hunt?'

'Nothing,' Jake said glumly.

Morgan had parked the Land Rover and was walking over to them.

Gavin called out to him. 'Oh, by the way, Morgan, I left my backpack down at the waterhole yesterday. I wouldn't be too bothered over it, except that there's something rather valuable in there.' He glanced awkwardly at Jo. 'It's something I wanted to give you tonight, for our anniversary. I thought we'd still be on the trail, you see.'

Jo was pleased. 'That means we'll *have* to do the trail one day soon so that we can retrieve my gift. Perhaps after we've been to Zanzibar.'

As the next part of their holiday in Africa, the Achesons had booked into a resort on the famous tropical island that lay just off the coast of Tanzania.

'The situation in the wilderness might be back to normal by then,' Jo continued, giving Morgan a hopeful glance.

'I wouldn't count on it,' said Morgan.

Jake seized his chance. 'You could get the rucksack

back today.' He turned to Morgan. 'Let's drive down in the Land Rover to get it.'

Morgan looked uncertain. 'Better if we radio to Johnson and see if he can find it.' The camp staff were still in the wilderness area, having spent the previous day packing up the camp.

'But we know *exactly* where it is,' argued Jake. 'And anyway, Johnson and the others are probably halfway back with the donkeys already. Please,' he implored Morgan. 'We can be back in time for lunch. And you never know what else we might find while we're there,' he added darkly.

'I don't think we'll find anything,' came Morgan's sober response. 'Those shiftas are probably miles away by now.'

But Jake was not deterred. He felt an overwhelming sense of responsibility for the rhinos, particularly the three he'd come to know – Nina, Pea and Faru. Musabi was supposed to have been a sanctuary for them, but it had turned out to be the exact opposite. Jake wouldn't rest until he knew the rhinos were safe again. He threw down his trump card. 'You're supposed to be responsible for the guests on the trail, aren't you, Morgan?'

Morgan nodded, his eyes narrowing as he tried to guess what Jake had up his sleeve.

'That must mean helping them to get back things they'd lost,' he went on stubbornly.

Morgan grinned. 'You're a persuasive guy.'

'So, how about it?' Jake pushed further. 'Are we going?'

Morgan sighed. 'I suppose so. But just to the waterhole and back again.'

'Are you sure?' asked Gavin. 'I mean, I don't want to put you to any trouble.'

'It's no trouble. As Jake said, we can go down in the Land Rover. It'll only take us an hour, as long as Jake doesn't want to go looking for the poachers,' said Morgan.

'I don't,' Jake said truthfully. He was more interested now in finding the rhinos.

Minutes later, Jake and Morgan were in the Land Rover. Morgan had just turned on the ignition when Rick appeared at Jake's window. 'Going somewhere?'

'Er, yes,' Jake said. 'Gavin left his backpack at the waterhole.'

'And you kindly volunteered to fetch it for him?' Rick's tone told Jake that his stepdad knew exactly what he was trying to do. 'I take it you've finished cleaning the pool?'

'Not quite,' Jake confessed. 'But I will when we get back.'

'Right,' Rick said, then added warningly, 'You're looking for a backpack, Jake, not poachers.'

NINE

'Do you think the poachers could be locals?' Jake asked as they drove slowly along the rough emergency track.

'They're more likely to be from other parts of Tanzania, or even from countries like Kenya and Congo,' answered Morgan. 'You know how much people around here value Musabi.'

Morgan was right. Those who lived in the villages surrounding the game reserve were very protective towards it. They understood that the more successful Musabi was, the more employment opportunities there would be for them.

'Maybe the *shiftas* come from even further away, where rhino horn is actually used,' Jake speculated. And then, as if a light had been switched on in his head, he blurted out, 'Hey! That's it! The poachers must be from the Far East. That's where the biggest market for powdered rhino horn is.' His words tumbled out in a rush. 'And who's staying in Musabi and showing lots of interest in the black rhinos? Mr Cheng, Mr Samsudin and Mr Lin!'

Morgan shook his head. 'Steady on, Jake. You're putting two and two together and making not four, but four thousand!'

'No, really,' Jake persisted. 'Think about it. They turn up here, excited as anything about tracking black rhino. They're even more excited when they see Nina and Pea. Then, as soon as we get back from the trail, they vanish for a few days and in that time, we find the murdered rhino. Next thing, Mr Cheng pitches up alone and he tells us the other men are still away on business. What kind of business, I wonder?' he finished sarcastically.

Morgan still wasn't buying Jake's argument. 'You've been reading too many detective stories. You know very well that their business is the lodge development.'

A pair of bushbuck burst out from a thicket next to the track and bounded away from the Land Rover.

'Except that Mr Cheng is now backpedalling and saying that maybe they won't build the lodge after all, because according to him, the bush is too dangerous for his guests.' Jake sat on the edge of his seat. 'The lodge is just a front, Morgan. Can't you see that? The men only pretended they were going to build it so we wouldn't suspect them of being the poachers.'

Morgan remained unconvinced. 'I don't think so, Jake. And you're making very serious accusations.'

He stopped the Land Rover next to a game path that cut across the track. Switching off the engine, he looked at Jake over the tops of his sunglasses. 'Those three men *are* here on business. You saw the architect's plans yourself. And anyway, I know that Mr Cheng has already been telling people in Sibiti that the lodge will mean many jobs for local people. Would he have made such a promise if he didn't mean it?'

Jake shrugged. 'I don't know.' A tiny voice inside him said, *They're probably false promises, like everything else. Mr Cheng's just leading the people on to cover up what he's really doing.*

Morgan continued. 'I suggest you don't say another word about your crazy theory. The last thing Musabi needs is for people to start accusing us of slander.' He climbed out of the Land Rover and slung his rifle over his shoulder. 'Come on. The waterhole's not far from here. We'll fetch the backpack and be on our way again in ten minutes.'

Walking behind Morgan through the bushes, Jake thought about what the ranger had said and began to have some reluctant second thoughts. In the peace of the undisturbed bush, things took on a new light. Poachers were normally incredibly secretive. What poacher would be bold enough to hatch a plan like the one Jake had described? *It would be just a bit too obvious*, Jake admitted. *And those three men are really nice*. The more he thought about it, the more he realized that his imagination had been running away with him. It was just that he was so desperate for the poachers to be caught.

Jake was relieved to find the backpack where Gavin had left it, on the ground next to the flat rock where they had sat while waiting for some action at the waterhole. *Jo will get her anniversary present after all,* Jake thought with pleasure as he hoisted the bag on to his back, then turned to follow Morgan back through the dense bush to the emergency track a few hundred metres away.

Their route skirted the place where the rhino lay dead, but Jake felt he had to have a last look at the shocking scene. It was as if, deep down, he feared that the poachers had rigged up another lethal trap across the game path.

With Morgan walking a short distance ahead of him, Jake thought he'd be able to slip away for a moment without the ranger even noticing he'd gone. All he wanted to do was get a little closer so that he could see from a distance if everything was all right.

He rounded a clump of bushes. About fifteen metres in front of him was the game path that the ill-fated rhino had used to reach the waterhole. The two strong trees that had served to anchor the snare stood out on either side of the well-used track. Jake half expected to see another thick wire strung between them, but to his relief, there was nothing. The path was safe.

'Thank goodness,' Jake sighed. Satisfied, he retraced his footsteps until he could see Morgan again.

Walking about fifty metres ahead, Morgan glanced over his shoulder at Jake trailing behind him. 'What's up? Tired?'

'No. I just slipped behind a bush for a few seconds,' Jake replied, being rather economical with the truth.

Very soon, the Land Rover came into view. Jake noticed a jackal sniffing round the tyres. He wondered if the little dog-like animal had ever seen a vehicle before since this was almost the first time one had ever been this far down the emergency track. In other parts of Musabi, the animals were so used to cars they didn't regard them as a threat, which was why people on game drives often saw more than those who went on foot. In the open, nothing masked a human's scent, so that the animals with their super-sharp senses could pick up the presence of people from a long way off.

As if to prove this, the jackal jerked up his head and sniffed the air. His beady eyes spotted Morgan coming towards him and he instantly turned tail and trotted away through the bush.

From somewhere to one side came a sharp hissing bird call. *Ksss, ksss. Sik, tsk. Ksss.*

Jake saw Morgan glance in the direction of the calls. He looked back as half a dozen brown birds burst out from the bushes a little way behind him. Chittering loudly, they flew directly towards Jake, their red beaks tiny flashes of colour against the green leaves. *Red-billed oxpeckers*, he identified them. He had often seen these birds pecking ticks and dry skin off the backs of large animals like buffalo and rhinos.

Jake felt the blood drain from his face. *Rhinos! Oh no!*

'Run, Morgan!' he shouted, and in that very instant he saw an unmistakable dark grey shape emerging from behind a bush to one side. The rhinoceros stamped the ground, then gave an angry snort.

'It's going to charge!' Jake yelled.

In a flash, he scrambled up a tree, and that's when he saw not one, but three black rhinos. Two adults were sniffing the air and pointing their ears in Morgan's direction as they tried to identify what their keen senses had picked up. The third rhino was a baby. Wearing a puzzled look on its little face, it stood just behind its mother, instinctively sniffing the air as well and moving its outsize ears like radar trying to pinpoint a signal.

Jake knew the mother and her calf at once. 'Nina and Pea!' Despite the tension, he was conscious of a feeling of relief at seeing them alive and well. There was also no mistaking the biggest rhino. Faru's extra-long lower horn acted like an identity card.

There were no trees near Morgan so his only choice was to make a run for the Land Rover. He sprinted towards it as if he was running the race of his life and flung open the front door just as Faru stormed out from the bushes.

Jake held his breath, desperately hoping this was yet another mock charge, a warning from Faru not to come any nearer to the calf and its mother. But Faru was in deadly earnest and thundered straight on.

Morgan glanced over his shoulder then leaped into the driver's seat, slamming the door behind him before Faru could reach him.

The enraged rhinoceros galloped to the Land Rover, his head held low to thrust his mighty horn into what he thought was his enemy.

Jake heard the engine start up then cut out immediately. Morgan must have stalled it. He dug his fingernails into his palms while he waited for Morgan to try again.

At last the engine roared, but Morgan had wasted precious seconds. In a heartbeat the rhino reached the Land Rover and with a fury that seemed almost insane, he rammed his horns into the side. There was a sickening crunch of metal being buckled and Jake's immediate thought was that Faru was going to hurt himself.

But Faru just shook his head and charged again. Jake felt sick. He could see Morgan desperately trying to start the engine for a third time, a look of panic on his face. But it was too late. With another mighty thrust, Faru pushed the vehicle right over. *Thud!* It landed on its side, dust billowing up around it.

'Morgan!' Jake yelled.

There was no movement inside the vehicle.

Angrily, Faru lunged at the Land Rover a final time, buckling a front wheel, before whirling round and crashing back through the bush. Jake saw Nina and Pea running away too, and in the blink of an eye all three rhinos had disappeared.

Jake was too shocked to move. Desperately, he waited for Morgan to emerge from the battered Land Rover. 'Morgan,' he shouted 'Are you OK?'

Silence.

At last, Jake felt the strength flowing back into his body and he slid down the tree trunk. Landing on the ground, he glanced round nervously, keeping his fingers crossed that the rhinos really had disappeared. Then he ran across to the overturned Land Rover, his heart pounding wildly.

He hauled himself up on to it and even before he'd yanked open the door facing upwards, Jake knew that Morgan was badly hurt. He could see the ranger crumpled up against the shattered window on the side that lay flat against the ground.

Panic gripped Jake. He pulled the door open and reached inside. 'Morgan! Grab my hand. I'll pull you out.'

Morgan groaned. 'I can't move.'

Jake went cold. 'What do you mean, you can't move?' he demanded, his voice cracking.

'I think I've broken something.'

Jake stared at his dad's right-hand man. His left arm lay limply on his ribcage and his legs were folded beneath him, as if they were bent in two. There was a jagged cut on his forehead where he must have hit the windscreen. Blood trickled out from the wound, oozing down Morgan's face and seeping into his shirt sleeve.

Morgan struggled to lift his head. 'You've got to go for help,' he appealed to Jake, his face twisted with pain.

Go for help? That would take ages. And by the time Jake returned, Morgan could be in a much worse state. Already he looked as if he was in shock, for his eyes were half-closed.

Jake hit his head with one hand. 'Think!' he ordered himself. He clambered down to the other side of the Land Rover and tried to shove it back on to its wheels. He pushed his back against it and heaved, willing a super-human strength to take hold of him. But despite the adrenalin flowing through him, he couldn't budge the vehicle a centimetre.

Fear tightened itself around him like an icy hand. He climbed back on top of the Land Rover and peered in again. 'Morgan! Stay with me,' he cried, realizing that the ranger's eyes had closed. 'Don't pass out.'

Jake stood up with one foot on the buckled front wheel. 'Help!' he screamed at the top of his voice, but even as his desperate cry rang through the air he knew no one would hear him, no one but the birds and animals hidden in the bushes around him.

'Someone! Help!' Jake screamed, his voice breaking.

He had never felt so helpless in his entire life. He looked at Morgan again, hoping against hope that he'd come to and would be able to suggest something. 'Morgan!' he sobbed, hysteria bubbling up inside him. 'Wake up, please! Tell me what to do.'

Morgan lay still, the blood trickling out of the cut on his forehead.

Jake's eyes fell on something sticking out behind Morgan's back. 'The radio!' Jake gasped with relief as he recognized the short aerial. Carefully he manoeuvred himself into the back seat before leaning over and easing the walkie-talkie out from behind the unconscious man's back.

He clambered out again, then pressed the button on the two-way radio. Dispensing with the normal procedure, he simply called for help. 'It's Jake. We've had an accident. Come quickly.'

Jake waited for the radio to crackle to life. Seconds passed, then a minute. It could have been hours. 'Help! Morgan's badly hurt,' Jake screamed into the radio as if by raising his voice, he would make himself heard.

Silence.

Jake pressed the talk button again. 'Come in, someone. Anyone.'

Still silence. No one was listening. Or, which was more likely, the radio had been broken in the impact when Faru sent the Land Rover crashing to its side.

Jake tugged at his hair in frustration. And then he saw Morgan's rifle on the floor of the Land Rover, half-hidden by his legs.

Gingerly Jake eased himself into the front and reached for the gun, his hands slippery with sweat. He hauled himself out again and went to stand a short distance from the Land Rover.

'Please let this work,' he prayed. He pointed the gun up into the sky, closed his eyes tightly and pulled the trigger. It was the first time he'd ever fired a gun in his life. The blast shattered his ears and he staggered backwards as the gun kicked in his arms. At the same time, flocks of startled birds flew out from the treetops, their shrill cries of alarm competing with the ear-splitting crack of the rifle.

Jake braced himself and fired again. Then again, and again, until he'd used up all the bullets. Exhausted, he collapsed on the ground and, with his head buried in his hands, he prayed harder than he'd ever done in his life that someone would hear the shots and come to investigate.

TEN

Jake didn't know how long he stayed like that but suddenly he became aware of the most welcome sound he'd ever heard. Voices. And they were right next to him.

He looked up. 'Herbert! Kwanza! Thank goodness, you found us.'

'The whole world could have found you after all that shooting,' said one of the guards, eyeing the rifle that was still in Jake's hand. 'And luckily for you we weren't too far from here.' He looked at the overturned Land Rover in front of them. 'Has someone gone for help?'

'No. Morgan's trapped inside,' said Jake, jumping to his feet. 'He's badly hurt.'

'Why didn't you say so?' said Herbert, running at once to the vehicle.

It took twenty minutes for the two guards and Jake to lift Morgan out of the Land Rover. In that time, Morgan came round again but he was in such pain that Jake almost wished he'd lapse back into unconsciousness.

When the injured man was lying on the ground, his head resting on Herbert's jacket, Jake crouched down next to him. 'I'm sorry, Morgan. It's all my fault.' His voice caught in his throat as he fought to hold back tears.

The game guards were trying to get the Land Rover back on to its wheels. Jake ran to help them even though he was reluctant to leave Morgan's side. The sooner they were back on the road, the better for the injured game ranger.

'Moja, mbili, tatu,' Kwanza counted, and, with muscles straining and their boots slipping on the ground, the three of them heaved and pushed until, at last, they righted the heavy vehicle.

'Let's see if we can get it going,' said Herbert, sweat rolling down his forehead. He climbed into the driver's seat and turned the key that was still in the ignition.

The strong roar that came from under the bonnet was as welcome a sound to Jake as the guards' voices had been half an hour earlier.

'Let's get out of here,' said Kwanza.

As gently as they could, they settled Morgan on the back seat. Then, with Herbert at the wheel and Jake and Kwanza sharing the other front seat, they started back for the house.

Jake kept thinking it was a miracle that Herbert and Kwanza had heard the gunshots. *Imagine if they hadn't,* he thought and shuddered at what might have happened then.

But for Morgan, the crisis was far from over. With the Land Rover's front wheel buckled and the track as rough as any in the savannah, the journey was extremely bumpy. Leaning over the seat to keep an eye on Morgan, Jake could see how agonizing the drive was for him, as he winced in pain every time they hit a bump or went round a tight bend. *I hope the journey won't make his injuries worse,* Jake prayed. On a first-aid course he'd done when he still lived in England, he had learned that it wasn't a good idea to move a person who'd been hurt. But in this situation, they'd had no choice.

'Not long now,' Jake tried to comfort Morgan.

When they were within range of the house, Kwanza radioed to Rick and told him what had happened. Even though Rick's voice came back indistinctly, Jake could hear that he was both worried and angry.

'It sounds bad. I'll get on to the medics right away,' he said.

Along with his terrible guilt, Jake realized he was going to be in big trouble with his stepfather. While Rick hadn't exactly said Jake couldn't go into the wilderness to get the bag, he'd obviously been unhappy about it. He must have known that the whole thing was Jake's idea in the first place.

And it was, Jake admitted to himself, wishing he could turn the clock back. *I'll just have to face the music.*

Rick, Hannah and the Achesons were waiting for them at the top of the drive. As soon as Herbert turned off the engine, Hannah opened one of the back doors. Jo stood close by with a first-aid kit.

Jake climbed out and stood to one side, watching helplessly. He hardly dared to look at Rick who was leaning in through the other back door, talking to Morgan.

Hannah offered Morgan a bottle of water and gently held his head while he took a few sips. 'We've called the medical rescue helicopter,' she told him. 'It'll be here in a few minutes so I don't think we should move you until then.' She looked over her shoulder at Jake. 'Fetch a blanket, please. Morgan's in shock and we need to keep him warm.'

Glad to be able to do something, Jake sprinted across to the house, nearly tripping over Bina on the way. He scooped up the little antelope and carried her indoors, shutting her in his mum's office. She'd be safe there when the helicopter landed.

He chose the softest blanket from the linen cupboard then ran back outside, climbed into the front of the Land Rover, and passed the blanket over the seat to Hannah. Jo was leaning in from the other side, gently dabbing the wound on Morgan's forehead, and Gavin was just behind her, holding the open first aid kit, his sun-reddened face creased with worry.

Rick was standing next to the Land Rover, examining the buckled front tyre. 'Beats me how you managed to drive back here with this,' he said to Herbert.

'There was no spare,' said the guard and Jake

remembered that Morgan had taken the other wheel to Sibiti to be repaired yesterday.

Morgan moaned as Jo carefully washed the wound with disinfectant then placed a soft dressing on it. 'This will probably need a few stitches,' she said, making Jake feel like the worst person in the world.

He got out of the Land Rover and looked up at the sky, impatient for the helicopter to arrive. Rick came to stand next to him but said nothing. In a way, his stony silence was a lot worse than if he had read Jake the riot act.

Jake wished the earth would swallow him up. 'I'm sorry,' he murmured when he couldn't stand Rick's silence any longer. 'Really I am. I shouldn't have made Morgan go.' He turned away, not wanting everyone to see the tears that were rolling down his face.

Rick put an arm around Jake's shoulder. 'OK, OK, Jake. You *are* a bone-headed fool and you do some crazy things at times. Still, from what Morgan managed to tell me, this was an accident.'

'No, it wasn't,' croaked Jake. 'It was my fault.'

'Actually, it was mine,' came Gavin's voice and Jake felt another hand on his shoulder. 'I left the backpack at the waterhole, and I mentioned it to Morgan.'

'I should have minded my own business and just kept cleaning the pool,' Jake mumbled. 'I didn't even do that properly.'

A distant chopping noise sounded in the sky. 'I can hear the helicopter,' Jake said, lifting his head, and before long, he spotted the red and white chopper skimming above the tree tops.

Rick ran across to a flat area of the lawn and signalled to the helicopter to land there. The others kept well back and Hannah quickly closed the doors and windows of the Land Rover so that the dust churned up by the rotor blades wouldn't add to Morgan's discomfort.

The rescue chopper dropped neatly on to the grass and even before the rotor blades had stopped swishing round, a paramedic opened the door and jumped out with a large orange-coloured box in one hand. She was followed by the pilot who carried a stretcher and a small oxygen tank. Keeping their heads down, they ran across the lawn and spoke quickly to Rick.

He led them to the Land Rover, then stood back while the paramedic attended to Morgan. She pulled on a pair of latex gloves before checking Morgan's blood pressure, and his breathing and heart rates. Next she shone a small bright light into his eyes, then slipped an oxygen mask over his face before putting a drip in his uninjured arm. She also checked the gash on his forehead and seemed satisfied with Jo's temporary dressing.

Finally, with the help of the pilot, she eased her patient out of the Land Rover. They carefully transferred Morgan to the stretcher, his neck supported by a special cushion.

Strapped to the stretcher, with the mask covering his face and an intravenous line feeding fluids into him, Rick's right-hand man looked more badly hurt than ever.

I'll make it up to you one day, Jake vowed silently, swallowing the lump that rose in his throat.

The rescue team lifted the stretcher and carried Morgan across the lawn. The others followed at a short distance.

'We'll visit you in hospital,' Hannah promised as the stretcher bearers gently hoisted Morgan into the helicopter and slid the door shut. She caught Jake's eye and gave him a sympathetic smile which made Jake want to burst into tears again. Everyone was being so *nice* to him!

To make matters worse, his mum came over and gave him a warm hug. 'The main thing is that Morgan's safe now. And so are you.'

'Thanks, Mum,' said Jake, feeling the lump in his throat get even bigger.

The pilot climbed into the cockpit. Moments later, the motor started to whine. But there came too, another urgent engine sound. It was a car roaring up the drive at top speed.

Jake stared at it in astonishment, because instead of stopping in the parking area, the small green car bounced across the lawn and headed straight for the helicopter.

'It's Shani and her mum,' he said when he

recognized their faces behind the front windscreen. 'And Leona,' he added, surprised to see her in the back of the small vehicle.

The car screeched to a halt right in front of the helicopter. The doors flung open and the passengers tumbled out. 'Is Morgan already inside?' Mrs Rafiki asked breathlessly, and before anyone could reply, she was at the door of the helicopter, peering in through the glass.

Shani brushed past Jake and gave him an angry look. 'Why did you have to go back to the wilderness area?'

'I, er . . .' Jake stammered, then gave up. Shani didn't wait for his answer but, like her mum, ran to peer in through the helicopter window.

'She's pretty mad,' Leona explained to Jake. 'But that's just because she got such a fright when we heard what had happened to her uncle.'

'How did you find out?' Jake asked.

Mrs Rafiki, who was tall like her daughter, was signalling frantically to the pilot and trying to tell him something above the noise of the rotor blades.

'Your mother told us about it,' said Leona. 'Mrs Rafiki came to fetch Shani and me because we were going to spend the night at her house, but we'd only just arrived when your mum phoned with the news. So we jumped straight back in the car.' She raised her eyebrows. 'Mrs Rafiki can sure drive fast!'

'Just as well,' muttered Jake as the chopper door

slid open again and Shani and her mum climbed inside. Jake assumed they wanted to check on Morgan before he was taken off to hospital. But they weren't just checking on their relative. Jake soon realized they were going with him!

Mrs Rafiki appeared briefly in the open doorway, tossed her car keys to Rick then ducked back inside as the paramedic pulled the door shut again.

The whine of the motor grew more intense and the rotor blades gathered speed. Rick dashed over to the small green car and quickly drove it out of the helicopter's way. The down draft from the rotor blades stirred up a mini-storm of dust and bits of loose grass that pelted the onlookers who beat a hasty retreat across the lawn.

'It's good that Shani and her mum can go along too,' remarked Leona as the rescue helicopter lifted off the ground, hovered for a moment above the house, then banked to the left and chopped through the air on its way to the hospital in Dar es Salaam.

'I guess,' was all Jake said in reply. Digging his nails into his palms, he watched until the helicopter had disappeared. *I hope Morgan's going to be OK,* he prayed, while deep down inside him a niggling fear arose that the ranger's injuries could be a lot worse than they seemed. What if he never walked again?

The cut on his forehead didn't look too serious, but his legs had looked pretty mashed, back in the overturned Land Rover.

ELEVEN

In the silence that followed Morgan's departure, Jake suddenly remembered that he was still carrying Gavin's rucksack. Somehow in all the drama, he'd managed to keep it on his back. He took it off and gave it to Gavin.

'Thanks,' said Gavin. 'But it comes at a hefty price.'

'Absolutely,' agreed Jo, looking rather uncomfortable.

'Perhaps,' Rick put in. 'But this whole incident might just have an up side – if you can call it that. Because of the rucksack, we might yet get those poachers.'

Jake was taken aback. 'How?'

'What actually happened when you came across Faru?' Rick asked Jake. 'Did you surprise him, or threaten him in any way?'

'Definitely not,' Jake replied, feeling a bit hurt that Rick could even think he'd do such a thing. 'I'm sure he and Nina and Pea knew we were there long before we saw them. It was a bit like an ambush, really. Faru only charged when Morgan had walked past him.'

'Which tells us one thing for certain,' Rick commented. 'The poachers are still down in the wilderness.'

'What?' Jake gasped, while around him the others gave Rick puzzled looks.

Rick folded his arms. 'It's a guess, but one I'd bet on. You see, I reckon the rhinos are feeling threatened and that's putting them on edge, which is why Faru stormed the Land Rover.' He paused, then said quietly, 'The poachers might even have snared another one.'

'No way!' Jake blurted out.

Rick nodded sombrely. 'I think we're dealing with some very professional people here, people who can vanish off the face of the earth even with skilled trackers going after them. If you and Morgan hadn't gone down there today, I might have been none the wiser. So, like I said, there is a positive side to the accident.'

'Does that mean the guards will start looking for them again?' asked Jo.

'Yup!' Rick told her. 'After they've had a couple of nights' rest.'

What if something happens in the meantime? Or if another rhino's lying suffocating in a snare? Jake's frustration levels soared. 'But that might be too late,' he said to Rick.

'It's a risk we'll have to take,' his stepdad replied sombrely.

The group on the lawn split up. The Achesons went to their chalet to pack because they were leaving early the next morning for Zanzibar. They were sad to leave, but said they'd definitely be back within the next few months.

Going across to her own chalet, Leona looked rather lonely and forlorn. With her new best friend flying by helicopter to Dar es Salaam, her father having gone out to meet someone again, and his colleagues still away on business, she had no company at all.

Jake briefly felt sorry for her, even to the extent that he nearly went after her to invite her to come for a swim, but he decided not to. He had far more serious matters on his mind than Leona. She'd just have to amuse herself like she usually did, by listening to her personal stereo or making a long-distance call to Lawrence.

Inside the house, Hannah asked Jake if he'd like something to eat. 'You missed lunch,' she reminded him.

'I guess I am hungry,' he admitted, aware of his rumbling stomach but not sure that he had an appetite.

Hannah brought out a bowl of fruit salad and put a dollop of ice cream on it, then made a pot of tea for Rick and herself.

They went out to the patio, but on the way Jake heard a scratching coming from inside Hannah's office. 'Oops! Bina.' He'd clean forgotten about her shut away in there.

He let her out and she trotted along at his side, looking up at him almost accusingly.

'Sorry, little B. But I've got lots on my mind today,' he said. 'Like Morgan being hurt and the danger the rhinos are in at this very minute.' It was no good! The poachers *had* to be caught, and fast. Their presence in the wilderness was like a ticking time-bomb that threatened the delicate balance in Musabi.

If it hadn't been for them, Morgan wouldn't be on his way to hospital now, Jake thought. At the same time, he felt a wave of sympathy for Faru. No one could blame the rhino for charging Morgan. The animal had acted out of a deep instinct to save himself, and possibly Nina and Pea too, after he'd felt threatened in his new home.

Out on the patio, Rick was pouring tea.

'Why don't *we* go and see if you're right about the *shiftas* still being around?' Jake asked him. He sat down next to Rick and half-heartedly dug his spoon into the bowl of fruit salad.

Rick looked at him in disbelief. 'Say that again?'

'We could go down and see if we can find anything.'

Rick must have momentarily forgotten about the teapot he was holding, because he kept pouring even though the cup was full. The tea spilled out, overflowing the saucer and swamping the table. 'I can't believe I'm hearing you right. Even after what's just happened you still want to go on a shifta hunt?'

'Watch out!' said Hannah, taking the teapot from Rick.

Rick jumped up to escape the tea streaming down from the table on to his lap.

'Sorry,' Jake said. He seemed to be doing an awful lot of apologizing lately, but he wasn't about to give up. And then he had a brilliant new idea. 'Hang on! You know the tracking device? We could take it down to track the rhinos and make sure they're safe. Until now we've kind of chanced upon them, or they've come across us. But with the tracker, we could find them easily. And we could do a stake-out.' His words spilled out almost as uncontrollably as the tea had done. 'If we keep monitoring the rhinos, we might bump into the poachers.' They'd been doing things the wrong way round all along. The best way to catch the poachers was to get to the rhinos before they did.

Rick looked too astonished to say anything. Hannah seemed stunned as well. She folded her arms and looked at Jake with her blue eyes very wide.

Eventually Rick spoke. 'You're a madcap, Jake.'

'No, really. Think about it,' Jake insisted. 'You know how you're always telling me that to track an animal, you should think like one?'

'Yes . . .' Rick's tone was guarded.

'So to track a poacher, you must think like one?' Hannah put forward.

'Exactly!' said Jake. 'Only, with the transmitter, we can be one up on the *shiftas*.'

The tea had stopped dripping from the table so Rick sat down again. He bent his head to take a sip from his overfull cup, then gave Jake a sideways look. 'You know, I don't think it's such a crazy idea after all. It might just work.'

Jake jumped up from his chair, bumping the table so that the cup wobbled wildly, spilling another wave of tea. 'Let's go!'

Hannah rolled her eyes. 'I give up!'

'It's worth a try,' Rick admitted. 'And after what happened to Morgan, I'm more keen than ever to catch those criminals.'

'Then are we going?' Jake pressed.

Rick and Hannah exchanged a glance then Rick sighed. 'If we don't, I'll never hear the end of it.' He looked at his watch. 'But we can't go now. It'll be dark in a few hours. First thing in the morning, we'll take the jeep down to where Faru charged Morgan and set out on foot from there.'

Jake was disappointed that they couldn't start at once, but at least Rick had agreed to his plan. 'Great!' he said. 'I'll fetch the receiver and get some food and water packed now so that we don't waste a minute tomorrow.'

Blip, blip, blip. The signal being picked up by the tracking device that Jake held out in front of him was faint but steady. It indicated that somewhere, not a million miles away, was a rhino.

Jake and Rick had been on the rhino's trail for about ten minutes. To Jake it seemed like the ultimate twenty-first century way of finding a wild animal. 'Much better than looking for dung and spoor,' he said.

'It's OK for times like now,' Rick agreed. 'But it's not the real thing you know.'

'Blow the real thing,' Jake said, although he couldn't deny that he really enjoyed the times he and Rick went tracking in the bush.

The signal grew stronger and led them past a waterhole, through a papyrus swamp, across a plain, past another waterhole and into a dense grove of tamboti trees. By now the bleeps were so strong that Jake was convinced they'd come across the rhino at any moment. He looked at Rick, who nodded as if he'd read Jake's mind, then the two of them went on, treading so silently that they moved like shadows, their breathing the only sound apart from the bleeps.

Moments later, Jake heard another quiet drawing in of air, this time from a little way in front. It reminded Jake of the breathing sounds that Nina had made when they came across her on the first wilderness trail just days before.

Rick had heard it too. With the slightest movement of his head, he indicated to Jake to keep still.

They waited tensely, peering through the trees.

Jake wondered which rhino they had found. Perhaps it was Nina and Pea, or Faru again.

And then, like a ship silently appearing out of the mist, the bulky grey shape of a rhino suddenly loomed out about twenty metres in front of Jake. And it *was* Faru.

The enormous creature that had so nearly killed Morgan stared straight at Jake, his ears pointing forward. Jake's heart skipped a beat, but then he noticed something different about the rhino. He seemed strangely calm, not wound up like the last time Jake had seen him. There was no stamping of the ground, no threatening snorts.

Faru stood utterly still, gazing at Jake, then quite unexpectedly he dipped his head, turned round and ambled away. Jake was dumbfounded. Faru could have easily charged him and Rick and flattened them in a moment. Could it be that, deep down, the rhino was just a quiet animal that simply wanted to be left in peace to mind his own business?

And you have every right to be left in peace, Jake said silently. *You shouldn't have to fight for your survival.* He felt a knot of anger tightening in him. With the black rhino on the brink of extinction, man, its greatest enemy, was still persecuting the magnificent beast.

But Faru *was* going to survive, and so were Nina and Pea, and all the others in the wilderness. Jake was more determined than ever to help Musabi's precious rhinos.

And then it struck him that the signals were as strong as before, even though Faru had moved off. Perhaps there was another rhino close by.

Rick realized this too. 'We've hit the jackpot,' he whispered as he and Jake started in the direction of the bleeps, which was somewhere to one side of Jake and Rick, at a right angle to the direction Faru had taken.

They followed the electronic impulses deeper into the tamboti grove and had gone only a few paces when Jake picked up the faint aroma of a fire. Just ahead, a thin plume of smoke was rising into the air.

'Someone's lit a fire,' he mouthed silently to Rick, a shiver running down his spine. Could it be the poachers? Or was it just the remains of a fire the guards had lit?

Treading even more lightly than before, Jake and Rick moved through the trees. They came to a small clearing and stopped dead. Three men were lying curled up asleep next to a dying fire. Rifles lay beside them, while nearby was a heap of wire coils. It was all the evidence Jake needed.

The shiftas! He wanted to punch the air in triumph. He gave Rick a look of victory and his stepdad gave him a thumbs-up. 'We *have* hit the jackpot,' Rick whispered.

They gingerly approached the men, Rick holding his rifle at the ready. Something else struck Jake. The bleeps were stronger than ever. *That's funny,* he thought. The closer they got to the men, the clearer the signal. It was as if the poachers were wearing transmitters themselves.

And that's when Jake practically tripped over the answer to the riddle – a yellowy-white pointed object sticking out of a brown canvas bag on the ground, right next to the heap of wire. A rhino's horn, still with the transmitter inside! It must have been from the animal snared at the waterhole.

There was justice in the bush after all. Jake was almost beside himself with jubilation at the way things had worked out. The thing the poachers had murdered for had led Jake and Rick straight to them.

Rick grinned. He was obviously as amazed as Jake at how the three *shiftas* had been caught in their own trap. Then his face became serious again and he signalled to Jake to switch off the receiver. Jake obeyed at once, realizing he should have switched it off a lot earlier. It was sheer luck that the pulsating noise hadn't woken the men up.

Rick silently gathered up the poachers' rifles and stashed them behind a bush on the far side of the clearing while Jake kept a close eye on the sleeping men.

'Time to wake them up,' Rick whispered, going over to the poachers. He bent down and put a hand on one man's shoulder.

Feeling Rick's touch, the man moaned and rolled over. He had a long narrow face with sharp features and dark, almost black eyes and hair. He looked up at Rick and instead of jumping up in fright as Jake expected, he whispered faintly, 'You've got to help us.'

'Yes, to go to prison,' said Jake.

The two other men were also moaning but made no attempt to get up. Jake was puzzled. Why didn't they jump up and look for their guns to defend themselves? At least put up some sort of fight, or try to escape?

He frowned at Rick, but his stepdad didn't look puzzled at all. Instead, he looked rather amused.

'What is it?' Jake asked.

'These *shiftas* haven't been sleeping,' Rick explained, his eyes twinkling. He pointed to the fire. 'They used tamboti logs and the fumes have made them ill. They probably feel so rough they wish a rhino would come and trample them and put them out of their misery.'

Jake grinned. The poachers had really run out of luck!

'Right, you lot,' said Rick, taking another one by his arm. 'On your feet. I know you're feeling terrible, and you probably need medical attention. But the only way that's going to happen is if you come back with us.'

Meanwhile Jake checked inside a couple of other brown canvas bags lying next to the one containing the slain rhino's horn. There was nothing interesting in them, just some clothes and food and, in one, a small tub of ointment.

The screw-topped jar looked oddly familiar to Jake and he searched his mind for a clue. Just as the answer came to him, Rick exclaimed, 'Mr Samsudin!'

Jake spun round and instantly recognized the tall, distinguished-looking man standing next to Rick, his head drooping either from shame or because he felt so ill.

In a rush, lots of what Mr Samsudin had said and done came back to Jake. His curiosity about every aspect of rhinos, from their dung to what habitat they preferred; the difference between them and white rhinos; the extensive notes he took about everything. Jake even remembered that when Rick had explained about tamboti wood being poisonous, Mr Samsudin had been fetching his diary from his tent. *Just as well he didn't pick up that tip*, he thought.

'How *could* you?' Jake blurted out to the man who had been his parents' guest.

Mr Samsudin seemed too weak to reply. He looked at Jake through half-closed eyes then groaned quietly and dropped his head again.

Jake hadn't yet seen who the third poacher was. Could it be Mr Lin, or Mr Cheng? When Rick pulled the man on to his feet, it turned out that he was a stranger, with features similar to those of the first man.

While the poachers leaned against the trunks of

trees, too ill even to think of making a run for it, Jake helped Rick to kick soil over the embers of the fire. Then they gathered up the men's belongings and Faru's horn.

'Right. Let's go,' Rick ordered. 'Jake, you lead and I'll walk behind where I can keep an eye on everyone.'

Jake glanced over his shoulder at the pale, shivering men who stumbled after him. 'Serves you right,' he muttered unsympathetically. A long, tough walk through the bush in the heat was a great way for the wilderness to get its own back!

TWELVE

It was mid-afternoon when Jake and Rick returned to the house. They'd already been back once to pick up the Land Rover, then driven the three men to the nearest police station where they were placed under guard while they recovered from the tamboti poisoning. As soon as they were well enough, they'd be taken to court.

'Now let's find out just how much the other two men are involved,' said Rick as he parked the Land Rover. He was clearly referring to Mr Cheng and Mr Lin. 'I reckon they're probably heading a horn-trafficking syndicate, although it beats me why Mr Samsudin should have been doing the actual poaching himself. Normally, the ringleaders leave the dirty work to locals who know the bush well. But I guess we'll soon find out.'

To Jake's disappointment, the men weren't back from their so-called 'meetings'. Leona said they were due to return around dinnertime.

Jake agonized over what they could be up to.

Hunting down rhino by themselves? But Rick said that was extremely unlikely, and Jake had to admit that the idea of fussy Mr Lin being involved in the gory details of a poaching operation seemed impossible. It was more likely that the pair were arranging for the trafficking of the horn to the Far East. Perhaps they were even negotiating with local *shiftas* to trap rhinos in other parks now that the Musabi game guards were on full alert.

Jake's impatience made it impossible for him to wait for the men to return. He decided to sound out Leona to find out what she knew. So when Rick went to his office, Jake stayed at the chalet with Leona.

'Er, Coke?' she offered, opening the bar fridge in the small sitting room. She seemed surprised that Jake should want to spend some time with her after all their disagreements.

Jake nodded. He felt rather awkward and wasn't sure how to go about getting information from Leona. He couldn't just blurt out what he and Rick had discovered that afternoon. Rick wanted to confront Mr Cheng with the news first.

Jake took the ice-cold can from Leona then the two of them went out to the patio at the back of the chalet.

'Hey look! A chameleon,' Jake pointed out, spotting the goggle-eyed little reptile clinging to a branch right next to the patio.

'What a beautiful bright green,' Leona enthused.

The chameleon fixed one eye on Jake and Leona,

while the other kept watch on a flying insect hovering a few inches in front of it.

'Keep still for a second,' Jake whispered. 'Let's see what his next move is.'

The chameleon edged forward jerkily, folding his hand-like feet around the branch. He stopped again and anchored himself by grasping the branch with his tail. Then without warning he shot out his long tongue and caught the insect. The way the chameleon swiftly recoiled his tongue reminded Jake of the way the electric cord shot back inside the vacuum cleaner.

Leona grinned. 'That's so neat!'

'Yeah. Now watch this.' Jake gently eased his hand under the chameleon until it was clinging to his fingers. As they watched, the reptile, angry or afraid at being handled, changed from a brilliant uniform green to a blotchy greeny-black.

Leona's eyes opened wide in amazement. 'Now I know why unreliable people are sometimes called chameleons. You don't really know their true colour.'

'You said it,' said Jake, seeing the perfect opportunity to steer the conversation round to Mr Samsudin. 'I haven't met a lot of human chameleons. Have you?'

'No. Just one or two.'

'Your friends or your parents' friends?' Jake probed.

Leona frowned. 'I don't know. I *think* my friends are all OK. Also, my mum and dad's friends.

Otherwise they wouldn't be friends, would they?'

'You mean like Mr Lin and . . .' Jake paused for the briefest moment before saying darkly, 'Mr Samsudin.'

'Uncle Andrew's definitely not a chameleon,' said Leona. 'He's my mum's brother and I've known him all my life. He's so predictable, I could even tell you what he'd choose from a menu.'

'And Mr Samsudin?'

'Mmm. I don't know him that well. My dad just met him a few months ago when he was looking for another business partner for the lodge project. He seemed perfect because he knows a lot about Africa. He's been here a lot.'

'Really?' said Jake, feeling his heart beat faster. 'Do you know why?'

'I never really thought about it,' said Leona. She sat down on a cane sofa and sipped her drink.

Jake couldn't keep the secret to himself any longer. He had to find out just how much Leona knew. So what if he told her what had happened? She was going to find out soon enough anyway, and Jake could stay with her until her dad came back so she wouldn't have a chance to warn him. Also, Rick had probably already tipped off the police about Mr Cheng and Mr Lin. There was no chance they'd be able to skip the country, even if they found out about the others being arrested.

Jake took a deep breath. 'Mr Samsudin comes to

Africa to poach rhino horn,' he said, watching Leona closely for her reaction.

'Rubbish,' Leona said at once. Then, as if she'd suddenly remembered something, she added, 'He deals in African crafts and artwork. I know he sometimes goes to the Yemen on business trips.'

'Well, I can tell you for sure that he's not buying or selling art there, or anywhere else,' Jake persisted. 'And I bet you know that only too well yourself,' he added.

Leona looked thoroughly confused. She put her Coke on the table next to her and leaned forward, folding her arms. 'What's up with you, Jake Berman? You've disliked me from the day I got here. Now you're telling me some wild story about a man my father trusts.'

'Mr Samsudin *is* a poacher,' Jake said, then told Leona the full story.

Leona was dumbfounded. She could only shake her head in astonishment.

'And now the finger's pointing at your dad and uncle too,' Jake confessed.

Leona sprang to her father's defence, her eyes flashing. 'There's no way Papa would *ever* do anything like that. Nor would Uncle Andrew. They're both honourable men. Can't you see that?'

Jake nodded. 'I *thought* they were.' They'd seemed really nice on the Wilderness Trail. But then again, he'd once liked Mr Samsudin too.

Leona leaned over and grabbed Jake's arms. 'Look, my dad's *crazy* about animals. Wild ones especially.'

'And Mr Samsudin?' Jake persisted.

'He's going to the Yemen again tomorrow . . .' Her hands flew up to her mouth. 'Oh my,' she gasped. 'That's it!'

'What?'

Leona didn't waste time explaining. Instead she jumped up and pulled Jake back into the sitting room. 'Look at this!' She grabbed a colourful book off the coffee table. Jake caught a glimpse of the title before Leona flipped the book open. **THE YEMEN**, spelled the bold capitals.

'This is Mr Samsudin's book. He was reading it the night we came here, and I was just having a look at it this morning.' Leona breathlessly turned the pages until she found what she was looking for. 'There!' she announced and passed the book to Jake.

He frowned. 'It's a picture of some knives.'

'Ceremonial daggers,' Leona corrected him. 'Look what the handles are made from.'

Jake scanned the article that accompanied the picture. His heart skipped a beat. The handles were fashioned from rhino horn. Then, as he read on further, he learned that rhino horns were so valued for making the handles that just one horn alone could fetch tens of thousands of dollars. Perhaps even as much as sixty thousand. The slain rhino's horn, and any other he could get his hands on, were worth a vast fortune to Mr Samsudin. More so than any share in any tourist lodge.

'We must tell Rick,' said Jake, and now it was his turn to grab Leona's arm as he ran out of the chalet and over to his stepdad's office.

As far as Jake was concerned, there was only one way to celebrate cracking the horn-poaching syndicate: by re-opening the Wilderness Trail.

Rick agreed, but only after sending Herbert and Kwanza to check on the rhinos' mood. The guards tracked the animals with the same device that had caught the poachers, then returned to say that Faru and the others seemed quite relaxed.

In his mind, Jake experienced once again the moment just before the poachers had been found; the moment when he and Faru had faced each other head on in the tamboti grove. *He was relaxed even then,* Jake reminded himself. *Maybe he sensed that time had run out for the men who were out to harm him and the others.*

When Mr Cheng and Mr Lin heard what their colleague had been up to they were outraged. They denied having any part in the evil scheme and showed Rick documents they'd signed that same day proving they'd been buying land about twenty kilometres away from Musabi.

It turned out that Mr Samsudin was a big-time trafficker of not only rhino horn, but elephant ivory too.

'He doesn't usually get his hands dirty with the actual poaching, but after his usual team was caught in another game park just a few days before he arrived here, he had to recruit two others very quickly,' Rick reported. The police had phoned him with what they'd learnt from questioning Mr Samsudin. 'He had contacts in Dar who arranged for him to meet the two new poachers.'

'But that doesn't explain why he went down to the wilderness himself,' put in Hannah.

'I guess he wasn't sure he could trust the new men, and wanted to see for himself that they weren't going to keep any of the poached horns for themselves,' Rick suggested.

'That's rich,' scoffed Hannah. 'Someone like him accusing others of being untrustworthy!'

'I guess it takes a thief to know a thief,' remarked Rick. Then, turning to Mr Cheng and Mr Lin, he apologized to them. 'We shouldn't have lumped you with Mr Samsudin.'

'But it was the logical thing to do,' Mr Cheng pointed out reasonably. 'He was with us.'

'And we *are* from a country where rhino horn is used to treat various ailments,' said Mr Lin. 'Not that I'd ever use them myself, of course.'

Jake suddenly felt sick. 'Do you think that jar of cream had rhino horn in it?' he asked, remembering how Mr Samsudin had given it to Rick to put on the lantana scratch.

'Oh no,' said Mr Cheng. 'That came from a very skilled herbalist whom I use myself.'

'That proves even more that we shouldn't jump to hasty conclusions,' said Rick.

Mr Lin brushed the issue aside. 'Think nothing more of it. And anyway, it is we who should apologize to you for bringing such a, er, snake into your midst.'

'Or chameleon,' put in Leona, winking at Jake.

'I think that's being a bit harsh on the chameleon,' said Mr Cheng. 'They're not treacherous creatures in the least.'

'All the same,' said Rick. 'To make sure there are no hard feelings, I'd like you all,' he glanced at Leona, her dad and Mr Lin in turn, 'to come on the celebratory wilderness trail free of charge.' Then turning to Hannah, he added. 'You as well, love. It's time you experienced it too.' And before Hannah could protest, he told her that he was organizing a ranger from a neighbouring reserve to hold the fort at Musabi for a few days.

'In that case, I hope we see Nina and Pea,' said Hannah. 'I'd like to take some shots of them for my portfolio.'

Even though the hiking group was already bigger than the six people normally catered for, Shani was going along too. She'd come back to Musabi from the hospital in Dar es Salaam the day after Morgan was admitted saying that he had broken a leg and that his collarbone had needed surgery. This meant he'd be in hospital for a couple of weeks but he would make a complete recovery after that.

Jake was hugely relieved. He couldn't have lived with himself if Morgan's injuries had meant he'd never walk again.

'He was looking his old self when we left him,' Shani reassured Jake, then added with a chuckle, 'Mum told him that he didn't have to go to so much trouble to get a bit of time off.'

'Well, I'm going to give Morgan some real time off,' Rick said warmly. 'Not just the time he needs to recover, but as much as he wants to take a well-earned holiday.'

'He'll never do that,' Shani said at once.

'Why not?' asked Leona. 'If I were him, I'd live it up in the city or on a beach somewhere for as long as I could.'

Shani frowned. 'Well, you're not him. Uncle Morgan's life is in the bush. Especially here, in Musabi.' She turned to Jake. 'Isn't that right?'

'A hundred per cent right.' Jake smiled, then added, 'It's my life too.'

'And mine,' said Shani. 'And I can't wait to go on the Wilderness Trail.' Her eyes sparkled, and Jake knew that, like her uncle, she was her old self again, the one who would always be more interested in the ways of the wild than the city.

* * *

Two days after the arrest of Mr Samsudin and his two sidekicks, who turned out to be skilled trackers from the Yemen, clever enough to hide from Rick's men but ignorant of the dangers of burning tamboti branches, Rick led his party into the wilderness area. Jake was at the back of the line, standing in for Morgan. He proudly wore the Musabi khaki uniform, complete with green epaulettes, that identified him as a ranger, albeit a temporary one. He felt a pang of regret that Jo and Gavin Acheson weren't around to go on the trail too, and resolved to e-mail them about it afterwards to tempt them back as soon as possible.

The trail was every bit as thrilling as the first one. Soon after they set out, Rick picked up the spoor of giraffes and they tracked the elegant animals to within a few metres. It was Leona who spotted the calf, a tiny giraffe still so wobbly on its legs that it could hardly stand up.

Shani was not to be outdone in the game-spotting score. Around mid-morning, she heard something and alerted Rick. They all stopped to listen, and Shani excitedly pointed to some creatures trotting swiftly across the plain about a hundred metres away. It was a pack of rare wild dogs.

'Well spotted,' said Jake, who had hardly ever seen the black and yellow painted dogs of Africa.

But it was Jake who alerted everyone to the

most thrilling sight of all. After lunch, they were approaching another plain when he saw something bounding through the long grass.

'Cheepard!' he whispered to the rest of the group.

The King Cheetah cub sprinted across the plain like an arrow, his gaze fixed on a hare streaking ahead of him. Behind him, sitting tall on an ant-heap, was Cheepard's mother, Kim, watching her cub with the pride of any mother seeing her child grow up to become what he was always meant to be.

'Isn't he awesome?' Shani murmured, her dark eyes shining.

Jake gave her a thumbs-up. The gesture meant a host of things, one of which was how good it was to see the cub where he belonged, on the open grassland rather than in a man-made enclosure. That's where he'd have ended up if Mr Sangoma, the witch doctor, had had his way and taken the cub back to his tribe. Jake always knew that Rick would never have allowed it, but in the end it was Mr Sangoma himself who decided to leave Cheepard in the wild.

At the end of the day, they reached the camp where Jackson Kupika met them with a tray of cold drinks and a bowl of macadamia nuts.

'You're a hero, Jackson!' Hannah said gratefully, pushing her long black hair out of her face before helping herself to a glass of freshly squeezed orange juice.

Later on, when they were settled around the fire

waiting for dinner to be served, there was a faint rustling in the shadows at the edge of the camp.

Leona, dressed in designer jeans and a black sweater that matched her shining hair, shuffled closer to the fire. 'I'm not taking any chances,' she said firmly.

The rustling came again. It sounded like a branch being shaken, only there wasn't a breath of wind. This meant it had to be an animal disturbing the vegetation.

Shani, who, unlike Leona, was wearing very ordinary jeans and a T-shirt, shot Jake a look. 'Buffalo?' she mouthed.

'Or rhino?' Jake whispered back. But then again, perhaps it was just an antelope, or a monkey nesting in the tree for the night.

The answer came a moment later when the animal silently stepped out from behind a tree. It wasn't any of the creatures Jake had considered. Instead, a large bull elephant stared silently at the group of humans sitting on the ground only metres in front of him.

Leona let out a strangled squeak as the elephant took a few steps towards them. Any closer, Jake knew, and the mighty five- or six-ton animal could trample them with the greatest of ease. But, despite the fact that elephants had gored two of the tents before the opening of the trail, Jake wasn't in the least concerned – unlike Leona, whose eyes were almost popping out of her head!

'Do something, Mr Berman,' she managed to whisper, only to be answered by Shani laughing softly.

'It's OK. He's only come to say hello.' Shani sounded as relaxed as Jake because they both knew the elephant well. He was Goliath, the semi-tame young bull that had been released into the wilds of Musabi after being hand-reared at Rungwa. It was his right-angled tusk that gave away his identity so quickly.

'Hi there, Goliath,' said Jake.

The elephant lifted his trunk and probed the air as if trying to sniff out something.

'Sorry, we don't have any bananas,' said Hannah. Bananas were Goliath's favourite treat.

Goliath dropped his trunk and looked at the group, his wise face creased with a knowledge of things that Jake could only guess at. Then he disappeared silently into the night, leaving Leona, her dad and Mr Lin speechless.

'I bet you never thought you'd get that close to an elephant in the wild and survive to tell the tale,' Shani teased Leona, who was as white as a sheet.

The startled girl could only nod and Shani added sympathetically, 'But you weren't to know. I'd have freaked if it had turned out to be any other elephant.'

'Me too,' Jake confessed. 'But I wish I'd taken a photo of you. We'd have been even then,' he chuckled.

'I think we are even now,' Leona smiled.

During dinner, Mr Cheng raised the topic of the lodge development. 'We'll be going ahead with *Safari World* after all,' he said. 'The more time I spend here, even with an elephant breathing down my neck, the more I know how much others from our city and beyond will relish the kind of experiences we've had. And we understand that the real danger came from the poachers, not the animals.'

Jake felt a stab of concern. He still had very mixed feelings about the lodge. On the one hand, he understood how important it was for Musabi and other reserves to draw more tourists. But on the other hand, the thought of huge brightly lit developments like *Safari World* spreading like some terrible weed across the savannah was unbearable.

Hoop, hoo, whoop. Hyena laughter surrounded the camp as it had done on the first night.

Leona looked across to Jake. 'Time to take a shower?' she teased.

'Sure. Off you go,' Jake retorted.

'We'll wait here with the camera for you to come back,' Shani joked, so that Leona's laughter almost matched the hyenas' for loudness.

Mr Lin had been rather preoccupied during dinner, every now and then scribbling hasty notes in a file he'd carried with him in his rucksack.

'Are you writing a diary of everything you've seen on the trail?' Hannah asked him.

The visitor looked up, his spectacles glinting in the firelight. 'Well, yes and no. You see, there are going to be major alterations to our plans on the basis of what we've learnt while we've been here.'

Major alterations! Jake didn't like the sound of that.

'You mean, like making the showers a lot more secure?' grinned Leona.

Mr Lin didn't get the chance to respond before Rick put up his hand and said, 'Sssh.' He was staring into the darkness beyond the camp.

Jake felt a shiver run through him. Rick was not one to be spooked easily. He peered into the gloom, forcing his eyes to detect the slightest movement while listening as intently as he could. And there in the shadows, he saw their next inquisitive visitor. It was a familiar bulky dark shape and as Jake had suspected, it wasn't an animal to be trifled with.

'Black rhino,' he whispered to Shani who was sitting on the ground next to him.

Jake didn't know how much the poor-sighted rhino could see in the dark, but one thing was sure: it would have heard and smelt them. The rhino turned its head to one side as if it was trying to pinpoint exactly where the human intruders were. Seeing the animal's profile in the starlight, Jake could just make out that it wasn't Faru, for its lower horn wasn't as long as his.

But he quickly realized who it was when he saw another movement just behind the rhino. 'Nina and

Pea,' he breathed as the smaller bulk of a calf loomed out from the dark, then bumbled forward a few paces.

Jake heard Nina make a sort of mouse-like squeak that was probably a warning to her calf not to go any further. Pea stopped and Jake saw her big ears prick up, then point towards him and the others as she tried to make out where the strange-smelling creatures were.

A large log that Rick had only just put on the fire caught light so that the flames suddenly flared up. In the brief brightness, Jake clearly saw Pea's face. The calf was staring straight towards him. She looked as if she was sulking, with her upper hooked lip slightly turned down, covering her lower lip.

Eek. Nina's call came again, and this time she gave her calf a gentle push with her head. Jake could have sworn Pea's top lip turned down in even more of a sulk as if she wanted to stay, but then the fire died down again and all he could see was the dark shape of the two rhinos in the shadows.

The pair stayed for a few more seconds then they turned and vanished into the blackness of the bush, just like Goliath a few minutes before.

Jake felt a deep happiness flood through him. Unlike the other times he'd seen the mother rhino and her calf, they had been utterly peaceful. It was as if they'd only come to view the humans in their midst, in the same way that the humans had come to see the rhinos. Perhaps, like Faru, they sensed that the poaching threat had been removed. Hopefully before long they'd come to believe that the journey from their old home was worth it, and that Musabi was a safe place to be.

Mr Lin was hastily scribbling more notes. 'That's it!' he said to himself. 'That's just the sign we needed.'

While the rest of the group looked at him with puzzled frowns, Mr Lin stretched over and passed the file to Mr Cheng. 'What do you think, Henry?' he asked, his eyes twinkling behind his thick glasses.

Leona's dad had been reclining on his cushion. Now he sat up, crossing his legs. He picked up a nearby lantern and held it over the file. A wide smile spread across his face. 'Perfect, Andrew,' he said. 'Just perfect.'

Jake's curiosity got the better of him. 'Can I have a look?' he burst out, and even as Jake's mum shot him a disapproving glance, Mr Cheng handed the file to Jake.

'By all means,' he said.

Jake geared himself up to protest against what he was convinced would be ideas for an even bigger development. But all he could do was gasp. Shani, who was leaning over his shoulder looking at the file too, also sucked in her breath. In front of them was a sketch of several small thatched dwellings hidden among trees, a bit like some of the villages in the rural areas of Tanzania.

'As you can see,' Mr Cheng explained, 'we have decided to tone things down.'

Mr Lin continued. 'And that's because we have learnt just how fragile the wilderness is. At first we saw only lots of space just waiting to be filled with buildings.'

'Does that mean you're not going to have a chain of lodges?' Jake dared to venture.

'Absolutely,' said Mr Lin. He paused to flick a bug off his sleeve. 'We're settling on just one which will be near Musabi. It'll still be luxurious inside, but as you can see, we want it to blend in with its surroundings.'

Jake leafed through the pieces of paper again. 'You've made a sketch of Nina and Pea as well,' he observed, admiring the simple but accurate drawing of the black rhino and her calf.

'Ah! As I said, they were the sign we were looking for.' Mr Lin looked across to where the rhinos had been. 'Ever since we decided to change the lodge, Henry and I have been searching for a new name, and an emblem.'

'Nina and Pea,' Jake breathed.

'That's right. The lodge will be known as Rhino Retreat, and Nina and Pea will be our mascots. Their images will be everywhere – embroidered on the linen, printed on the stationery and menus, etched onto glasses, painted on crockery. Even,' Mr Lin chuckled softly, 'painted on the walls of the shower.'

'Perhaps, Mrs Berman,' Leona's father suggested, 'we could ask you to take some photographs of Nina and Pea which we can use in our brochures and on our website?'

Hannah smiled. 'That would be a pleasure,'

Rick looked as relieved as Jake at the way things had turned out. 'Here's to a long and happy partnership with you,' he declared, raising his bottle of beer to the two businessmen. 'I promise we'll do our best to give your guests the ultimate wilderness experience in Musabi.'

'And I bet Uncle Morgan will warn them about the dangers of getting too close to an angry rhino,' Shani added.

'Yes. Even if its horn is worth a fortune,' Jake couldn't resist chipping in.

Leona had said nothing so far, but now she spoke up. 'You know, Jake, I think you might have hit on a good idea, about people learning things.'

'How do you mean?'

'I don't think people should come here just for a holiday.' Leona made a sweeping gesture with one arm that took in the campsite as well as the wilderness beyond. 'I mean, I've learnt so much in just a few days, and I just thought we were going to hang about to look at some animals then go home again,' she explained.

'What's your point?' asked her dad, looking at her across the fire.

'Children,' came Leona's simple response. 'We should have a special programme for school children. We can bring them out here so that they can learn about the wilderness. Just think, some of them have never even seen stars,' she finished with a glance at Jake.

Her dad folded his arms and said thoughtfully, 'You don't have the brains of a mosquito after all, my daughter. You have come up with something very important, something that will have great meaning for the future, for it is with the children that the future of our world belongs.'

'Indeed,' Mr Lin agreed, taking off his glasses to wipe them. 'We might even teach them that rhino horns are useful for one thing only.'

'And that's as a tool for the rhino himself,' Jake declared.

As he said this, he heard the distinctive snort of a rhino from somewhere in the bush. *Hrmph*. The snort was soft and low and carried no trace of anger. It was followed by an *eek*, the mother's call to her calf. Then came silence broken only by the chirp of crickets so that Jake was sure the rhinos had finally moved away. It was as if they'd been hiding in the shadows, waiting for the assurance they so badly needed, the assurance that all would be well in their new home.

This series is dedicated to Virginia McKenna and Bill Travers, founders of the Born Free Foundation, and to George and Joy Adamson, who inspired them and so many others to love and respect wild animals. If you would like to find out more about the work of the Born Free Foundation, please visit their website, www.bornfree.org.uk, or call 01403 240170.

HODDER

Another title from Hodder Children's Books

CHASE
Safari Summer 4

Lucy Daniels

Living on a game reserve brings Jake Berman face to face with animals in the wild. It's exciting – and dangerous – but Jake's always ready for adventure . . .

Some old friends from Hollywood have come to make a wildlife documentary on the Bermans' game reserve. When Jake discovers a King Cheetah cub living nearby, he can't believe his luck: this is the rarest type of cheetah in the world, and perfect for the documentary! But Musabi is suffering from a terrible drought and the cheetahs are in grave danger. Jake has to decide exactly how far he will go to help . . .

HODDER

Another title from Hodder Children's Books

HOWL
Safari Summer 6

Lucy Daniels

Living on a game reserve brings Jake Berman face to face with animals in the wild. It's exciting – and dangerous – but Jake's always ready for adventure . . .

Jake and Shani have won the chance to work on a conservation scheme for Ethiopian wolves! These rare and beautiful creatures are being brought close to extinction by the local community, who believe they are spreading rabies to local dogs. Suddenly everything goes horribly wrong, and Jake and Shani have a desperate fight on their hands to stop a rabies outbreak and save the wolves from being lost forever.